£11.95

A SPELL FOR OLD BONES

ERIC LINKLATER

A SPELL FOR OLD BONES

When the giants fell, old bones revived
Ogham inscription at Kirkseton

JONATHAN CAPE
THIRTY BEDFORD SQUARE
LONDON

FIRST PUBLISHED 1949

SFR
3.

F
372206

ISBN: A2406

PRINTED IN GREAT BRITAIN IN THE CITY OF OXFORD
AT THE ALDEN PRESS
BOUND BY A. W. BAIN & CO. LTD., LONDON

To

MARJORIE

for endurance

A SPELL FOR OLD BONES

CHAPTER ONE

THE two little fawn-coloured cows had been milked, and twitching their ears and flicking their tails against the evening flies they stood patiently at the gable-end of the house. Their large eyes of melting brown were as placid as the summer air, they paid no heed at all to the hoarse and frenzied screaming of the infant Furbister that daunted all human hearing with its greed. But the two milkmaids, rosy of face, bare-armed and bare of leg, looked at each other with a sad concern as they carried their beech-wood tub, frothing to the brim, into the house: and one said to the other, 'He'll be the death of her before her month is out.'

'He'll be the death of more than her,' said the other.

Karp, the father of the child, was standing at the door, and bade them hurry. He was a big man, rather more than ordinary height, but yet no giant; and now, stooped and distraught, he looked like a tall tree bending to a gale. He loved his wife — a big woman, too, broad of back, with a kind sweet nature and huge haunches — and only once had he watched her suckling their child.

'Hurry,' he said again. 'He has an appetite tonight.' Then he turned away from the house and walked quickly to the shore, where the sea was breaking bright and gently on the sand.

At the far end of the hall two women were rocking a pigs' trough, slung by straw ropes from the rafters. The infant Furbister was too big to lie in a cradle, like other children, so the pigs' trough had been scrubbed, and lined with moss and a few sheepskins, and so long as he was sleeping it served him well enough. But as soon as he woke he had to be tied down.

Doloroe, his mother, sat on a bench, and several other women stood about her, talking and trying to cheer her. Scattering the rushes on the floor with their heavy tread, the two milkmaids brought in their tub, and Furbister, as soon as he smelt it, stopped his screaming and began to yelp excitedly, like a greyhound when a hare gets up in the grass before him. His cradle was lowered to the floor, and the tub set down beside it. One of the women raised him, while another held a hollow reed in the milk and put the other end in his mouth. Gasping and slobbering like a leaky pump, Furbister began to suck, and in six or seven minutes the tub was empty.

'There now,' said one of the women to Doloroe. 'That's taken the rough edge off his hunger. He'll be quieter with you tonight, he won't torment you like he did at noon.'

But Doloroe, as she bared her breast, looked stern and sad, and Furbister, when the women lifted him to her lap, fell upon her as fiercely as a wolf leaping on a running hind. She was a generous mother, but she could not satisfy him, though he was swollen by the milk of two cows as well, and when he was taken from her he screamed as hoarsely as before. But now it was rage, not greed, that reddened his face and gave strength to his lungs, and there was hatred in his eyes.

'He will never forgive me,' said Doloroe, holding her sore and insufficient breasts with trembling hands.

'I cannot give him what he wants, and he will never forgive me.'

'He will forgive none of us,' said the oldest woman there. 'I have seen his like before, and those that grow up with a grudge against their mother's breast, carry a grudge against the world for ever after.'

They put him back in the pigs' trough, and hauled it up on the rafters, and rocked him till at last he fell asleep. But still they stood round him, and with foreboding eyes looked at the infant giant, belching in his angry dreams, who — if the old woman was right — might never forgive the world he lived in.

'They are a great nuisance, the giants,' said the old woman to Doloroe, 'but I am not blaming you, my dear, for it wasn't your fault that you bore him.'

At this time in Scotland, a little while before the Romans came, the occasional birth of a giant was the greatest inconvenience the people suffered. It was worse than the snow in winter, or drought in summer, or the great gales that made a fury of the sea in autumn and in spring. For the giants interfered with their neighbours, some for an evil purpose, and others — with much the same result — from the best of motives. There were few roads in those days, and because the lowlands and the valleys and the fertile straths were divided, the one from the other, by mountains difficult to cross, the people could not live in great communities, but only in small clans; and so their power of doing harm to each other was equally small. But the giants made nothing of the mountains, and sometimes, going from one clan to the other, would demand taxes from six or seven; or unite them all in a confederacy to make war on more distant clans to the east or the west.

The ordinary people were simple and contented with their lot. They were aware of their proper place in the great mystery of nature, and on the whole they believed what the Druids told them about Providence and the necessity of virtue. They were by no means perfect, of course. There were thieves and liars among them, the men were given to brawling, especially after they had been drinking, and the women to slander, mischief-making, and jealousy. There were girls who shed tears over their illegitimate babies, and young men and women who quarrelled with their grandparents. In every village, indeed, there were unwanted children, and very old people whom everyone wished to be rid of. There were brutal fathers, and stupid mothers, and vicious youths. Occasionally murder was done, from time to time there was a little fire-raising, the Irish settlers were somewhat given to cattle-maiming and other forms of revenge, and neither blackmail, rape, nor blasphemy was unknown. — But taking them all in all, the people were decently conducted, and considering their humanity their life presented a fair semblance of order.

The giants were different, however. They had enormous appetites, and were never satisfied. Because they were ten times stronger than ordinary men, they were contemptuous of natural laws and scorned the Druids. Some of them hated humanity and its world, while others, more benign but no happier, shook their heads over the imperfection of their neighbours, and tried to reform them. Which sort was the greater pest, no one could say; but if there had been many of either

8

kind, life would have become quite intolerable. It was the good fortune of Scotland that there were rarely more than three or four giants alive in any one generation; and even though, from time to time, a giant and giantess met, they never bred children of their own size, and indeed rarely bred at all. They were, it was thought, the last remnant of some older stock, whose unruly habits had destroyed it; and everyone hoped for their total disappearance in the near future.

News spread rapidly of the misfortune which had occurred to Karp and Doloroe, who were good people and much respected; and in all the pleasant lands that looked southward to the Solway, from the Rhinns of Galloway inland to Dumfries, there was, and would be for years to come, a great deal of talk about the devouring appetite of young Furbister, the destruction he caused, and the ill-temper that made him in his youth the terror of the countryside.

His mother lived longer than her women had expected, but she grew old and worn before her time, and died a week before the boy's seventh birthday, after a morning of summer storm in which a little ship had been driven ashore in Wigtown Bay, not half a mile from Karp's homestead. Two men, strangers in the neighbourhood, had escaped the wreck, and Karp had invited them to dinner. They gave him, in return for hospitality, news of a great calamity in the country of Carrick to the north; and while they told their tale, looked curiously at young Furbister. — There was a chief of Carrick, they said, living not far from the town of Ayr, whose wife, some six or seven years before, had given birth to a giant; and already the boy was inter-

9

fering with all who lived in that neighbourhood, and teaching old women — so they declared — how to suck eggs.

Doloroe grew pale as her linen apron when she heard that; but she said nothing, and continued to serve her guests, though now with trembling hands. Furbister sat at table with them, and behaved well. He was always interested in what strangers had to say, and would listen to them, when they talked of their own country, though he would listen to no one else. Now he leaned forward, eager and attentive, noisily supping a great bowl of soup. He was already a little taller than his father, his hands were enormous, and his huge feet, moving restlessly under the board, kicked the bare legs of a young woman who sat quietly with a red-haired boy beside her.

She also was a guest, a vagrant woman, but Karp and Doloroe were open-handed and turned no one from their door. She had been staying with them for a week or so, paying for her keep by helping the milkmaids and singing ballads after supper in a round and cheerful voice. She was a round and cheerful woman, good-natured but rather dirty, and when the twilight fell and she had done with singing, she could always be heard laughing and talking with some man or other under the gable-end of the house.

Her son was a sturdy, well-made boy, and in a country where rusty brown hair was the common shade, and black not unusual, a head as red as sunset and curling like a washed fleece made him conspicuous. He would have been handsome enough but for his left eye, which was rather bigger than the other; and that gave him a vacant and wondering look, like a natural.

He was quick-tongued, however, as lively as his mother, and because Furbister had taken a liking to him, he was not bullied by the young giant, as boys usually were; or very little. He was about the same age as Furbister, but no one had remarked his birthday or now remembered it, and even the Druids could not divine who his father had been; perhaps, it was sometimes said, because a Druid was in fact his father. All alone, by a little stream that ran into Loch Ryan, his mother had given him birth, and two days later she was on the road again, with her infant in a shawl on her back. His name was Albyn.

When dinner was done, Karp and the two strangers went down to the shore to see what they could save from the wreck, and Furbister and Albyn went with them. But Doloroe walked inland to a grove of oak trees where a Druid lived, and told him of the news she had heard from Carrick. She told him also of the fear she had, that this birth of giants, two in the same year, portended some great evil to their land. Not for twenty years or more had there been a giant in the southwestern parts of Scotland — in that broad triangle that points to Ireland, with the Solway Firth on the one side of it, and the Firth of Clyde on the other — and now, she said, with her voice unsteady and her hands fumbling at her skirt, here was a pair of them growing up. Would that not mean dark skies for Scotland and sorrow in its fields, she asked?

The Druid sat in his chair, with the tips of his fingers pressed together, and listened gravely. He had known for some time about the Carrick giant, he said, but not wanting to alarm his flock, when as yet there was no need for alarm, he had kept his knowledge to himself. The prospect was worrying, he admitted, and it was quite natural to regard it with concern. But there was no need to be unduly perturbed, and Doloroe, he said, must not give way to despair. For despair was a great sin, perhaps the greatest of all, and the proper way to avoid it was to say her prayers every night, and come to the Oak Trees every Sunday, where sound doctrine would reinforce her failing heart.

He talked long and earnestly, and did his best to comfort Doloroe, who was one of the worthiest of his parishioners. But he could say little to reassure her, though for his sake she made a pretence that he had said much. She thanked him and left a small present under the Oldest Tree, and then walked home again, uncomforted.

She gave instructions to her women about the morrow's work, and said her prayers, and went early to her bed. She fell into a light sleep and dreamed of youth, but woke again to unhappiness. It was dark now, but Karp was still at the shore, and there was no one to whom Doloroe could tell her trouble. So turning her face to the wall, she died.

CHAPTER TWO

IN the next ten or twelve years the red-haired boy Albyn and his mother wandered far and wide in the borderlands between England and Scotland, and while his mother made their keep with her jollity and songs, Albyn grew to manhood and observed the world about him.

It soon became clear that his nature was strong and wilful, and if his mother had been given to worrying she might have been worried indeed by his stubborn refusal to work, or to learn any useful trade. 'I am going to be a poet,' he would declare whenever he was asked to come and help with the peat-cutting or hay-harvest, with sheep-plucking, or the plaiting of ropes, or the thatching of a house.

'A poet?' the men would say, in wonderment and scorn.

'That's it,' he would answer, and go off to seek material for his verses by the side of a tumbling stream, or where girls were laughing together; where old men were talking, or the rowdier sort drinking.

At the age of twelve he had thought of becoming a Druid, for he had been much flattered by a sermon on the immortality of the soul. 'Your bodies are like the beasts of the field, and your deeds like the grass that the beasts consume. Take little thought of your bodies and do not vaunt your deeds, for they shall not long endure and tomorrow are of no consequence. But within the walls of a man's skull there is a treasure that does not die! Within the walls, in the very midst of the house, there is a little bone that is shaped like a little chair, and on it sits your Immortal Soul that shall live for ever.' — So said the priest, and when the service was over Albyn told his mother, 'I am going to be a Druid, for I must learn more about my soul.'

So he became the priest's servant, and for six months received instruction in anatomy, astronomy, herbalism, morality, and the Heavenly Providence. It was a great shock to him to learn, one day, that Providence had seated an immortal soul, on a little bony chair, in every human skull; for it had seemed to him, while he was listening to the sermon that so impressed him, that the priest was addressing him alone. It had pleased him greatly to be told that he, Albyn, had an immortal part — it confirmed, indeed, an inward feeling of which he had long been aware — but the idea that everyone was so distinguished seemed to him utter nonsense. He simply could not believe it, and telling the priest that his doctrine was quite implausible, and contradicted on every hand, he went off in a huff and rejoined his mother.

It was a year or two later that he fell in love with the moon, and perceived that nature intended him for a poet. He was lying half-asleep on a hillside when the moon came up through a fringe of birch trees, and wakened him. Never before, it seemed, had she come so close, and never had he been so private with her. He could see her roundness, the darkness closing behind her, and in her shining pallor he felt lost and faint.

She climbed the vacant sky, and he followed her aslant the hill until he came to a stream and in a pool perceived her image, not calm as in the sky, but tremulous as though, having fled and now been caught, she was a little frightened. There were some yellow irises growing by the pool, and picking them with unsteady hands, Albyn knelt down and laid them in the water. — For a few days he appeared indeed to be moon-crazed, he was silent and could not eat; but then his appetite returned, and he began to boast of his strange affection. 'A poet has many loves,' he would say. 'A nice little snub nose can please him for much of the time, but when he would sleep with his equals he lays his head on the breast of the sky.'

When he started to make verses, however, he was remarkably sensible, and took for his subjects, not the zenith and such-like enormities, but snub noses and the more attractive, though relatively humble, features of life.

He made many songs that his mother sang to shepherds and other lonely people, or to sailors in the little seaport towns along the Solway and on the coast of Northumberland; for they wandered from sea to sea. And then, being eighteen or thereabout, he declared that he could make no more verses of that kind, for they were unworthy of a true poet. 'And that,' he said, 'is what I have now become.'

So, having become a poet, he made no verses of any sort, but contenting himself with his own assurance, used it to condone all manner of irregular behaviour. Caught sleeping in the heat of the day, while others toiled, he would smile drowsily and explain his idleness: 'I am a poet.' — Caught sleeping where another had a better right to lie, he would offer the same excuse; and once or twice, among simple souls, it saved him from a beating.

Being a little drunk one night, he went courting his old love, the moon, near the grove where the Druid lived who, some half a dozen years before, had tried to teach him priestcraft.

'I am a poet,' he said, when the old man found him dancing and tumbling in the moonlight.

'Man goes upon two legs to keep his soul on high,' said the Druid, 'and for his soul's sake he should walk firm and upright.'

'But a poet falls upon his back to see the stars,' said Albyn. 'He must kiss the roots of things, and climb to forbidden windows, and dance to keep him supple. Only dullards walk straight and upright.'

'You lack reverence,' said the Druid.

'Not at all,' replied Albyn. 'I am what I am, I am resolved to continue so, and thus I show respect for what has been ordained.'

When he was twenty his mother decided to give up her vagrant ways and marry a swineherd who lived in the Ettrick Forest, on the hillside south of the river Yarrow. He was a dull man of surly temper, but he made a good living, and Albyn's mother, who was no longer as attractive as she had been, had begun to complain about her legs. Albyn agreed with her that, at her time of life, the most sensible thing she could do was to get married; and he would try, he said, to put up with his stepfather. On the morning after his wedding, however, the swineherd gave Albyn an iron pot, and told him to make a fire and boil water; for he had killed a pig and must singe and scald it.

'No, no, my dear man,' said Albyn. 'That's no occupation for me. I am a poet.'

'Then you can take yourself out of here,' said the

swineherd, 'for pigs is my trade, and pigs don't need poetry to fatten them.'

So Albyn said goodbye to his mother, and she wept to see him go, and he wept when he had left her. But the day was fine, and soon he recovered his spirit and resolved to march west into Galloway, to the country he had known as a boy.

He was in no hurry, for he had no business to speed him onward — he could be a poet wherever he was — and because there was no lack of hospitality in those days, he had little fear of going hungry. But usually he waited till an hour after sunrise before entering a house or a village to ask for his breakfast; for by then the men would be at work in the fields, and with only women to talk to he was the more likely to get lean bacon, and beans new boiled, and milk with the cream on it. He preferred men's company at night, when they had been drinking for a little while and were laughing after their work.

But though slowly, he moved steadily to the west, and after six or eight weeks came to Dumfries. There, in the broad street between well-built houses of turf or wood, he found, not women gossiping on their door-steps and girls yawning in the sun, but a frightened concourse of wives and mothers; old men, unregarded, chattering advice; and children crying, equally neglected.

He was at once surrounded by tear-stained women who besought him to go out and help defend them. An old man thrust a spear into his hand, another gave him a battered shield. 'Our men are out-matched, they will all be killed!' cried a big woman with wild eyes and hot hands. She took Albyn by the shoulders and shouted at him, 'You are young, you are strong! Go out, and fight on their side!'

'And be killed with all the rest of them?' asked Albyn. 'Oh no, dear ladies, that doesn't appeal to me at all. I'm not a warrior, you see, I'm a poet.'

'A poet should love glory,' said a tall girl with full breasts and a passionate mouth.

'I much prefer life,' said Albyn. 'But tell me why your men are fighting, and who is their enemy?'

'Furbister!' they cried, all together. 'The giant Furbister, who has come to conquer us and swallow our land!'

'I heard, about two years ago, that he had set up as a tyrant,' said Albyn, 'but I didn't know he was reaching out as far as this.'

An old man with two yellow teeth and purple lips told him: 'If he conquers here he will be master of all Galloway from the Irish Channel to the river Nith. He has proclaimed Glam, who was Chief of Wigtown, King of Galloway, and King he will be if the battle goes against us today. But Furbister will be his master, and ours.'

'And I knew him,' said Albyn, 'when he was a great, over-grown, lumpish boy with bad table-manners.'

'You have a spear and a shield,' said the tall girl. 'Come with me, and I'll show you where they're fighting.'

'Well,' he answered, 'it's really no business of mine, but I'd like to see what's going on. I make no promises, you understand — '

'Come,' said the girl, and taking his shield she led him by the hand, westward out of the village, and all the women cried their blessings on him as they went.

I am making a fool of myself, thought Albyn, I should have kept away from this. And he tried to make the girl walk more slowly, and even suggested sitting down under a tree to discuss the whole situation. But she was single-minded, fiercely intent on taking him into battle; and Albyn, beginning to lose his temper, guessed that her sweetheart was fighting with the Dumfries men. It was infuriating to walk beside a fine-looking, passionate girl whose thoughts were all on another man, and when they came to the field where the battle was raging, Albyn was disgusted by the noise of it, and by the hideous style in which the men on both sides had painted their faces to make themselves look fiercer than in fact they were.

It was a great battle, for Furbister's army was three hundred strong, and the men of Dumfries had had, to begin with, more than that. They had charged in line, but now their lines were broken and all over the field they were fighting in savage confusion. Furbister stood alone on a little hillock, and no one dared approach him. He had grown to his full height, of about two and a half fathoms; and even from a distance Albyn could see that he was more horribly and brightly painted than anyone else. But the noise of the battle was even more unpleasant, for quite near them were two men shouting with rage, another howling with pain, while sword screamed against sword or thudded dully on shield and skull. Flying greedily overhead, moreover, were flocks of buzzards mewing, kites whinnying, ravens grunting, carrion-crows groaning, and hoodie-crows croaking.

'There!' cried the girl, leaning excitedly against

Albyn, so that he felt the warmth of her body and the softness of her breast; and she pointed to her sweet-heart. 'Oh, go and help him!'

'He doesn't need any help,' said Albyn. 'He's getting on well enough.' For at that moment her sweetheart thrust his spear into the stomach of one of Furbister's men, and when his enemy went down, jumped on him and began to sing, as discordantly as the crows, a very foolish song of triumph.

'He looks so hot,' said the girl. 'He must be tired. Go and take his place for a little while, and let him come here and rest.'

'I'll do nothing of the sort!' cried Albyn. 'He's singing out of tune, so let him sweat. I'm going to talk to the one man here who does need help, and that's Furbister! He needs someone who'll talk good common sense, and tell him to stop making a fool of himself. — Give me that shield.'

He put his left arm through the loops on its inner side, and walking purposefully on to the battle-field, made his way towards Furbister. But when he was within forty yards of the hillock where Furbister stood, a wounded man, lying half-hidden in long grass, thrust a spear between his legs, and tripping him, brought him heavily to the ground. Albyn, in a great temper, leapt to his feet again, and with the haft of his own spear beat the wounded man cruelly about the head and shoulders.

'You fool!' he shouted. 'What do you mean by attacking me? I'm not one of your mutton-headed soldiery, I'm a poet! Can't you recognize a poet when you see one? No, of course you can't! You're too big a fool, like all the other fools on Furbister's side.

That's your trouble — you're fools! — and that's why you're such a nuisance in the country!'

'But I'm not on Furbister's side,' said the wounded man. 'I'm fighting for Dumfries.'

'Oh!' said Albyn. 'That makes it odder still. For the reason I was brought here — I didn't come of my own accord, I can tell you that — was to try and help Dumfries.'

'It's no help to break my head, as you've done,' said the wounded man.

'I'll tear a strip off your shirt and bandage it for you,' said Albyn; and kneeling down, took the Dumfries man's head on his knees. He was tying the rough bandage when a shadow fell across them both, and looking up he saw Furbister.

'Don't waste time,' said Furbister. 'You're not one of us — I can see that — but we're always glad to welcome volunteers if they fall into our way of doing things. And our way doesn't include taking prisoners. Either leave him to die, or slaughter him out of hand: that's your only choice.'

His manner was inoffensive, but his voice came rumbling out of the deep cavern of his chest like thunder from the clouds, and at close quarters his great painted face was unnerving. Albyn, for a reason he was not quite willing to admit, no longer felt so eager to talk good common sense to Furbister. It was hardly the time, he thought, to accuse him of folly and reprove him for insensate ambition. So he only said, in his mildest accents, 'I thought you might remember me, Furbister.'

'A man in my position meets so many people,' said Furbister.

'True,' said Albyn, 'and it's a long time since we met. It was in your father's house, when you were about seven years old, I think. My name is Albyn.'

'Indeed I remember!' cried Furbister. 'I thought I had seen that red head of yours before, and now — but of course I remember! We became great friends, didn't we? We played tricks together, you made me laugh, and I was very kind to you.'

'I suppose you were, in your own way.'

'And your mother stayed with us too. A pretty woman, but rather dirty, my mother said. My father and my mother are both dead now.'

'My mother has just got married.'

'Ah, marriage!' said the giant. 'I should like to talk to you about that. I'm in a difficulty at present, and to an old friend one can talk without reserve. Come home with me, Albyn, when the battle is over, and give me your advice. — I shall bring the battle to an end, it has gone on long enough.'

Furbister began to breathe deeply, to fill his cheeks with wind, and work his features into a terrifying scowl. His face was barred with red and white, a red stripe down the centre, white stripes on the cheek-bones, and his eyes were circled with deep blue.

'Why have you painted your eyes blue?' asked Albyn.

'It's considered appropriate,' said Furbister. 'That's how the Druids paint themselves when they're going to speak in the name of God.'

'I've got a good deal of authority myself,' said Furbister.

Then he uttered a warlike howl, brandished a great club, and with enormous strides advanced towards the

nearest group of the enemy. Within a few minutes
the men of Dumfries were in full flight, and Furbister was re-assembling his army to march into the
village.

The wounded man whom Albyn had assaulted was
now fairly comfortable. His head was well bandaged,
and he had used a strip of his chequered plaid to tie
up a deep cut in his thigh. Albyn gave him his shield,
to ward off the ravens and the kites and the carrion
crows, and told him to be patient. 'I must go now,'
he said, 'but your women-folk will be coming out
before long, I expect.'

Then he followed Furbister into Dumfries, where
he quickly learnt that the giant had offered peace in
the simplest of terms: his enemies must make full
submission and swear allegiance to King Glam of
Galloway, or he would put to the sword every man,
woman and child in the place, and burn their village
for a funeral pyre.

The men of Dumfries had no difficulty in making
their choice, but to preserve some dignity their Chief
and his Elders needed time for discussion, and so,
while the women brought food and drink, they sat
down with Furbister to consider his terms.

Albyn had to admit that the giant had learnt a
great deal about the business of being a tyrant. Despite
his hatred of the world and his fierce ambition, he could
now control his rage, as a singer controls his top notes,
and use it only when it seemed advisable. In council
his voice was not unpleasant, and his manner gracious
so long as his adversaries did not try to oppose his
rulings or bore him by the length of their speeches.
And he was not easily bored. Albyn grew tired of

speech-making long before he did, and on the following day left the council, yawning openly.

He happened to meet the girl with the fine figure and the passionate mouth, whose sweetheart had fought in the battle and was now in hiding. Her sweetheart, she thought, was still in danger of his life, and because she had seen Albyn talking in the friendliest way with the tyrant Furbister, her manner was most amiable and she readily agreed to walk in the fields with him. She begged Albyn to employ his influence on her sweetheart's behalf, and as Albyn knew that the Dumfries men had fully made up their minds to accept Furbister's terms, and the fellow was in no danger whatever, he promised that his life would be spared. But not without long hesitation did he commit himself, nor until she had used all her art and passion to persuade him.

By the time he consented, the night had given both of them so much satisfaction that they resolved to enjoy the rest of it where they lay, and trust the birds to wake them. The dawn was fair, they washed their faces in May dew, and a few hours later Albyn set off with Furbister and his army on their westward march.

The tall girl's sweetheart, a cautious and slow-witted man, remained in hiding in the hills for another three days; and though she married him soon after his return, he was hen-pecked from the start and lived a wretched life.

CHAPTER THREE

MOUNTED on sturdy, shaggy ponies that trotted briskly, Furbister's army was just able to keep pace with their long-striding leader. Furbister himself had to walk, because there was no beast in Scotland strong enough to carry him.

'This shows you how I live,' he said to Albyn, who was riding beside him. 'My people go in comfort, but I must march in the heat of the day. I am no better than a slave.'

'Why did you go to the trouble of making so large a kingdom?' asked Albyn. 'Big things are always a nuisance to carry.'

Furbister looked down at him with contempt and scorn, and exclaimed, 'Do you think I could have lived contentedly at the head of Wigtown Bay, surrounded by petty kings who thought they were as good as I, and were for ever plotting to seize our lands? They hated me, I hated them. They were short-sighted, mean, and selfish men, thinking only of their own good. But I had vision! I saw my destiny, and the destiny of all Galloway. And now they have vanished, those little men, and Galloway's a great kingdom.'

Albyn killed a horse-fly that had settled on his leg, and asked, 'Then why are you grumbling? If you've achieved what you set out to achieve, you ought to be perfectly happy.'

'I've a right to be happy!' cried the giant with passion in his voice. 'I deserve to be happy! But the world's so full of selfish people — people busy with their own ridiculous affairs — that I see no chance of happiness. I'm not appreciated as I should be, and that worries me. People aren't grateful enough, they don't seem to realize what I've done for them. Look at those children, for example.'

They were passing through a small village, and all its inhabitants had come out to cheer the victorious army. Furbister, on his eastward march, had ordered them to wear their brightest plaids and make flags to celebrate his triumph; but some of the children had lost their flags and dirtied their clothes, and now, sucking their thumbs or picking their noses, merely stood gaping at the cavalcade.

'They all heard my instructions,' said Furbister bitterly. 'They might have remembered their flags.'

At the next village he stopped and counted the people who lined the route. 'Seventy-two!' he said. 'There ought to be more than that.'

He summoned one of his officers and told him: 'There ought to be eighty here at least. Go and find those who're missing, and have them whipped.'

He strode on, and said to Albyn, 'Ingratitude's a horrible thing. Sometimes I think I'd rather trust my enemies than those who ought to be my friends.'

'But what enemies have you?' asked Albyn. 'I thought you had destroyed them all.'

'I am surrounded by enemies,' said Furbister. 'East of Dumfries, in the valleys of the Annan and the Esk, there are stubborn clans who still defy me.'

'But very small clans,' said Albyn. 'They're no danger to you.'

'All opposition is dangerous, and it shouldn't be allowed. There'll be no proper peace till I've wiped out every sign of it. Some day I must deal with the clans east of the Nith, and then, beyond the mountains, with Od McGammon and the kingdom of Carrick: they're all my enemies.'

'Tell me about Od McGammon,' said Albyn. 'Is he as big as you?'

'Some say he's taller, but I don't believe them. He's a soulless tyrant, he rules all Carrick with a rod of iron, but it's nonsense to say he's bigger than I am. He can't be.'

For some time they talked about Od McGammon, King of Carrick, the giant who had been born in the same year as Furbister, and like him had swallowed a score of petty chiefs to make a kingdom. Furbister did not approve of his methods, which were quite inhuman, he said. He affected to despise McGammon, but after they had discussed him for an hour or more, he fell into a gloomy silence; and then, bending his great head, he muttered hoarsely, 'It's *people* that prevent me from being happy! Stubborn, selfish people. But if Od McGammon were out of my way, and if — if — '

'If what?' asked Albyn.

'No,' growled Furbister. 'No, not yet. The time's not ripe to give you all my confidence. First you must prove yourself my friend. — Tell me, what sort of life do you lead?'

'I'm a poet.'

'A poet? I need a poet. I can use you in Galloway. Why, this is most fortunate!'

'How would you use me?'

'To celebrate my achievements, of course. I want an epic poem about myself and the creation of the kingdom. How long would it take you to make an epic?'

Albyn considered the question, and then replied: 'I should need, I think, about five years to contemplate the idea; another five to plan the poem; and then — though it's difficult to make an exact estimate — about ten to fifteen years to compose it.'

'What nonsense!' cried Furbister in a rage. 'If I engage you to make an epic, I shall expect to hear the finished work in three months' time.'

'You must look for another poet,' said Albyn, and whistled a jig-tune.

'Well, six months,' said the giant.

Albyn, still whistling, shook his head.

'If you can't finish an epic in six months, you should take up another trade,' said Furbister savagely.

'Grass grows quickly, and dies as soon,' Albyn replied. 'The oak tree takes twenty years to establish itself, but after three centuries people sit in its shade, and admire it from afar. If I were to compose a poem in your way, it would fade like cocksfoot; but if I make it in my own fashion, it may live like an oak. I make no promises, of course — but it may.'

Thinking deeply, Furbister paced slower and slower, and the army loitered behind him. From time to time he looked at Albyn with something like respect, and at last he said glumly, 'It's a long time to wait.'

'No longer for you than for me,' said Albyn, 'and the prospect doesn't worry me at all.'

They passed through several more villages, and Albyn grew very weary of the sound of cheering and the sight of people waving hurriedly made flags. Before darkness fell they halted for the night near Gatehouse of Fleet, whose inhabitants had been ordered to kill a great number of sheep and cattle, ducks and geese, to provide a feast.

'Poor people!' said Albyn, tearing apart his second duckling. 'They have to pay dearly for your triumphs.'

'They get a chance to show their loyalty,' said Furbister.

'And if they don't?'

'They are punished, of course. I can't let a few dissidents corrupt the majority.'

'They brew very good ale,' said Albyn with a sigh. 'They're better at brewing ale than waving flags.'

'It's a matter of practice, that's all. Have you tried the mead?'

'Yes — and I'd like some more.'

'Do all poets drink heavily?' asked Furbister.

'Very few of us can afford to.'

'That's not surprising, when you take twenty years to finish a poem.'

'My dear Furbister,' said Albyn, 'I believe we're going to get on very well together. You must tell me your other trouble.'

'Wait till tomorrow,' said the giant.

'Some years ago, when my mother and I were in Northumberland, I met a most unusual girl. I think you'd be interested — '

'No,' said Furbister, 'I don't want to hear about her. I've been disillusioned by women.'

'Wouldn't they help to pass the time, while you're waiting for my poem?'

'I was speaking seriously — and my guests aren't expected to be jocular till I pass the word.'

'Well, pass the mead, and we'll talk seriously about that.'

When Albyn woke in the morning, under a hedge-row full of wild roses, the sun was already high and small spiders had spun a web of gossamer about his hair, that obscured his vision. He brushed it away, and sitting up perceived that Furbister lay near him on the grass. The giant's hands were clasped beneath his head, he lay staring at the sky, and balanced on his enormous breast-bone was a small wicker cage in which a wren sat closely on her nest.

'What a pleasant picture!' cried Albyn. 'The least and loveliest poised upon the greatest and — well, upon the greatest!'

'I've been waiting here for an hour or more,' said Furbister. 'I want to talk to you.'

'But the wren!' said Albyn. 'Who gave you the wren?'

'A little girl, because I had been kind to her mother.'

'What a good start to the day!'

'Her mother is a widow, it seems. She had been told to kill six ducklings for the feast, and she brought only three. They were about to punish her, but when I heard of her fault I forgave her.'

'I'm beginning to grow really fond of you, dear Furbister.'

'A man in my position learns to show clemency from time to time. It's expected of him, and it pays if he doesn't overdo it.'

'Well, whatever the motive, the end was good.'

'And then the woman's daughter, crying in the silliest way because I had saved her mother's life, came and presented me with what she said was her greatest treasure: this wren in a cage. I don't know what to do with it.'

'Give it to me,' cried Albyn. 'I shall look for the grubs of butterflies and moths to feed her. I've often kept small birds in cages — but only for a little while, and then I let them go again. I had a pair of goldfinches once, but never yet a wren. How lovely she is, and how quiet!'

'I want to talk to you,' said Furbister.

'Where is your army?'

'They marched two hours ago, but we can catch them up. Put down the cage and listen.'

Furbister rose to his feet, and Albyn, for courtesy's sake, did the same. For a minute or so the giant stood brooding, then bending down he gripped Albyn beneath the arms and lifted him to the height of his own great face. He had washed the war-paint from his cheeks, but his eyes were still circled with dark blue, the colour the Druids used when they impersonated God.

He held Albyn so close that his gaze converged upon him in a squint, made fearful by his painted eyelids, and in a hoarse voice he exclaimed, 'Be honest — and tell me if I stink.'

'No more than might be expected,' said Albyn, who still felt queasy from the night's drinking.

'And what did you expect?' roared Furbister. 'A stench? Rank odours? Do you hold your nose if I come to windward? Do I infect the breeze?'

'No, no!' cried Albyn, as the giant raised him higher still, and seemed about to dash him to the ground. 'No, no, no, no! Set me down and I'll explain exactly what I meant!'

'Explain why your cheeks are pale,' said Furbister bitterly, and lowered him to the grass. 'Have you, like others, been sickened by the smell of my flesh?'

'You lifted me too high,' said Albyn, 'and I've a

31

bad head for heights: that's all that's wrong with me.'

He made an effort to regain composure, and went on: 'As for stinking, well, that's delusion, I do assure you. You wouldn't say that roses stink.'

'What have roses got to do with me?'

'Twenty roses are stronger than one rose,' said Albyn, and tried to overcome the slight nausea he had felt when the giant lifted him to the level of his mouth, and he saw the coarseness of his lips, the great pores in his cheeks, the rooty hairs in his nose; and smelt the odour of his skin, which was unpleasant. He gathered his wits, and continued rather desperately: 'You are twenty roses compared with the single flower of us lesser folk. You are a great beanfield, ripe in late July, whereas I am but a solitary plant. You are the whole harvest, golden in summer heat, while we small people are like a sheaf, an armful of oats, such as a sickle cuts. You smell of richness, we of poverty!' — And then, excusing himself, hurried to a ditch and vomited a little.

'You lifted me too high,' he repeated. 'I still feel giddy.'

Furbister's huge forehead, corrugated with thought, grew smoother. A little smile, of pleasure still half-ashamed, of gratification not yet secure, played shyly with his thick red lips. 'Twenty roses,' he muttered, 'a beanfield in July, the ripened harvest — yes, that may explain it all. It must — of course it does! No other answer's needed — and I'm too sensitive. I imagine faults, in myself and perhaps in others too, when there is no fault. A month ago, Albyn, I was ashamed and deeply hurt — I'll tell you the whole story now — for the King's daughter, old Glam's daughter Liss, fainted and fell ill because I lifted her to whisper in her ear a word that should, I thought, be private between the two of us.'

'A declaration of love?' asked Albyn.

'That was it.'

'Has she recovered yet?'

'No,' said Furbister. 'She's lost her power of speech, and I'm in half a mind to have no more to do with women. They are too frail for me. The scent of harvest — you have done me a great service, Albyn, for that was certainly the cause of her collapse — the scent of harvest is too much for them. A single sheaf, a sickle's cut, is all that she could bear.'

After a little while Albyn said, 'There is a girl in Northumberland, of whom I began to tell you last night, who might be strong enough for you.'

'No, no,' said Furbister. 'I don't want to hear of her.'

'She was only twelve when I met her, but already she overtopped all the men of that countryside. She was a fathom and a half high, sturdy as a brood-mare, black-haired, and ruddy cheeked —'

'Too late,' said Furbister. 'I am going to live celibate, like a priest.'

'She had a pretty turned-up nose, and a big mouth —'

'A coarse girl, a peasant's daughter,' said Furbister, 'and it is idle to talk of her. I'm not interested, and we've no more time for talk. The army's far ahead of us, and you must mount and I must march.'

He set off with great strides to the west, and Albyn caught his pony, which was grazing nearby, and with the bird-cage held in front of him, galloped in pursuit. There was no more conversation between them until,

33

about noon, they saw the army in front, marching in a thin cloud of dust.

Then Furbister abruptly said, 'That girl in Northumberland. She was going to be a big woman, was she?'

'A giantess, there's no doubt of it,' Albyn replied. 'A fathom and a half at twelve, broad as a peat-stack, handsome, good-natured, and growing fast. A girl of great interest — '

'But not to me,' said Furbister. 'There was a time — but no, not now. A man in my position can't set out to woo a stranger — and be rebuffed, perhaps.'

'Are you still in love with Liss, the King's daughter?'

'A doll!' said the giant contemptuously. 'A limp, disjointed doll. When she fainted in my hands, I forgot she had ever breathed.'

CHAPTER FOUR

A MILE beyond Wigtown stood the King's new palace, and Furbister's hall beside it. Their walls, of huge thickness, had been built of well-cut turf, there were wooden door-posts nobly carved, and sturdy beams supported a deep thatch of heather. Nothing so imposing had ever been seen in Galloway before, and most of the people who came, as if on pilgrimage, to stare at the palaces and contemplate their vast dimensions, were deeply impressed by their splendour and the power of which they were a symbol. But a few said they could see no necessity for such large buildings, and they did not suit the landscape. Furbister, like the majority, admired the great mansions, the plans of which he himself had drawn; but King Glam, with the minority, thought they spoilt the view. He was a mild and easy-going man, whose only real enthusiasm was the collecting of sea-shells, of which he possessed several thousand. Except for his shells and his motherless daughter Liss he had no deep affections — not even for himself — and he had acquiesced in Furbister's unruly ambition, and accepted the crown of Galloway, merely to avoid trouble. He had been quite happy as a small chieftain, ruling a few hundred people, and by leaving to Furbister all the responsibility of his vast new kingdom, he continued to be fairly happy still.

He was easily bored by ceremonies and speeches, but he sat his throne with natural dignity and could speak gravely and well without in effect saying very much. The celebrations that followed Furbister's victorious return went on for three days, but long before they were over the King was looking for shells on the beach, and Albyn had forsaken the drinking-hall to meditate, in solitude beyond the fields, on the sudden fever that had filled his heart with pain and desire.

He had seen, on a road by the sea-shore, the King's daughter Liss walking with two of her women, and she had looked at him, he thought, as he stood aside to let them pass, with the appeal of one who was a prisoner and desperately sought, in any stranger's face, for hope of rescue. He had heard already, in the earliest gossip of the palace, that all attempts to restore her power of speech had failed. Ever since the shock of Furbister's embrace she had been dumb as a stone; and her hands, they said, were as cold as a stone. Only her eyes were eloquent, and all they spoke was her distress.

In his wanderings in the borderland between England and Scotland Albyn had never seen a girl so lovely, so delicately fair; her body was supple and slim, her breast the very crest of perfection. — They had walked along the beach, she and her women, and Albyn, discreetly following them for a little way, had halted beside a footprint on the sand. She was walking barefoot, and the little print of her heel made his mouth dry and thirsty, as if it were an apple growing out of reach. — He could not sleep at night, and when morning came he could neither rest nor endure the conversation of other men; but walked all day on the hills, alone with desire and her picture in his mind.

When Furbister's victory had been properly celebrated, and the feasting at last came to an end, there were several days when everyone slept for much of the time, and in their wakeful hours quarrelled with their wives and avoided their neighbours. Then King Glam announced a day of prayer for his daughter, and in the evening there was a great concourse of people under the Oak Trees, where the Druids served their God. All the Druids from far and wide had assembled, the appropriate sacrifices were made, the proper hymns were sung, the priests chanted, the people groaned — and after three or four hours grew impatient and showed signs of restlessness. It was beginning to get dark, and the Princess Liss had not uttered a word.

Furbister stood sombrely on the outskirts of the crowd — Glam had asked him to keep well away from his afflicted daughter — and still the people waited, hoping for a miracle, but doubtful of it now. Under the Oldest Oak the Druids and the King conferred together in low tones, disconsolate and wholly at a loss; and Liss among her women wept.

King Glam said wearily to the Oldest Druid, 'You must tell them you have failed again.'

'It would be wiser,' said the Druid glumly, 'to explain the circumstances that prevent a cure: the people's continuing wickedness, their lack of faith, and so on.'

'Put it how you will,' said the King. 'You're unable to help my daughter, and so am I. But I would give half my kingdom — if it were mine to give, which it isn't — to restore her power of speech, and hear her voice again.'

Now Albyn had been standing in the forefront of the crowd, his famished heart feeding through hungry eyes on the beauty of the sad Princess, and when he heard the unhappiness in her father's voice, he took courage and resolved to do what a wild impulse had been urging him to do for an hour or more. The Oldest Druid had turned to the crowd and raised his hand for silence, when Albyn stepped forward and said, 'I have a medicine, sir, that may heal your daughter. Give me leave to try.'

'You are the poet, aren't you, who came here with Furbister?' asked the King.

'I am also, in my own way, a pilgrim. I seek knowledge, and I hope some day to catch a little glimpse of truth. I have travelled in all the borderlands of Scotland and England, and talked with many people. With men from the northern forests, from the islands still farther to the north, and even with one or two from Italy, who were runaways from the Roman army that is making war in the southern parts of England. But he who taught me how to cure certain ailments with the help of a small bird, such as I have here, was a native Scot, a wise man living under the Eildon Hills.'

Albyn held out, for the King's inspection, the wicker cage and the nested wren that Furbister had given him; and Liss, leaving her women, ran forward to look at it. From her dumb throat came a sound of pleasure, hoarse and strange, and she held her hands above the cage, her fingers curving as though to protect the sitting bird. She smiled, and looking upward from the wren to Albyn, was confused by the ardour of his gaze and his aspect of a simpleton. He was strongly made, he stood straight and square, his red hair shone in the last light from the west; but his left eye was bigger than its fellow, and though his other features were good enough, he had the wondering appearance of a natural. She was troubled by his gaze, yet held by it; not smiling now, but wondering too.

Glam watched them gravely, and inquired, 'How would you go about your cure?'

'Let loose the bird,' said Albyn, turning reluctantly to face the King. 'The bird will fly off to bring an herb of grace, and till it returns I must watch the patient and talk philosophy to calm her mind.'

'It seems to be quite an ordinary wren,' said the King.

'In its short life,' said Albyn, 'it has seen mercy, which is uncommon, and heard gratitude, which is most unusual.'

'This smells of magic!' said the Oldest Druid loudly.
'Have nothing to do with magic, sir.'

'Have nothing to do with the Druid!' shouted Furbister from the edge of the crowd; and all the Druids turned in his direction spitting like cats at a barking dog, for Furbister had long been their enemy. There were some in the crowd who laughed, some murmured angrily, and others waited in a nervous silence for what should next be said. But before the Druid could reply, the Princess in a high voice exclaimed, 'Oh!'

Now this was the first clear note she had uttered for many weeks, and from all the crowd came a sound like a long deep sigh, of hope and amazement. But Liss, and those nearest her, were staring at the wicker cage.

She had taken it from Albyn, to look more closely at the bird, and then, frightened by Furbister's rough voice, her fingers, jumping a little, had unlatched the door, and the wren had flown out. But in its nest lay a tiny egg, white and rose-spotted.

'Is that part of the cure?' asked Glam.

Albyn, more surprised than any of them, stared in perplexity at the egg; for he had not known that his wren was busy, and at first he could not think what to say about it. But Liss was close beside him, her shoulder to his, and her nearness stiffened his desire with resolution. Nothing should now prevent him, and suddenly there woke in his mind the boldest and happiest of ideas.

He spoke confidently to the King, there was even gaiety in his voice when he declared: 'This *is* the cure! The wren has gone to seek an herb of grace, and I shall stay beside the Princess to talk philosophy. Grace and philosophy are both required — but here's the medicine she must take.'

He went on more slowly, speaking with deliberation so that none should miss a word. 'What the wren has deserted, she must cherish. The bird seeks, and she must serve. When the wren returns, she shall reward, and before she speaks, the egg must live. Let her take it from the nest, and lay it in her navel, and give it her warmth.'

'While you sit beside her and talk philosophy?' asked the King.

'Without philosophy,' said Albyn gravely, 'nothing can prosper.'

'No, no!' cried the Oldest Druid. 'This is magic that he proposes, rank magic! It were better that the Princess remain dumb for ever, than be healed by magic!'

'I'm not so sure of that,' said the King, and Furbister, pushing his way through the crowd, exclaimed, 'Let my poet have his turn! The Druids have had their chance and failed, so now give him an equal chance.

He is a man, and the Druids, for all their pretence, are no more than that.'

'Blasphemy, blasphemy!' shouted the Oldest Druid, and all his priests began to sing the hymn they used for the rebuking of infidels. But Furbister's voice was almost as loud as their singing, and the ordinary people now supported the giant; for they wanted, very naturally, to see if Albyn's cure would work. Tempers grew fierce, and it looked as though there might soon be brawling. So to protect the Druids the King told his officers to disperse the crowd, and send both priests and people home; and when all had gone but Furbister and the Oldest Druid and some of his courtiers, he embraced his daughter and asked her if she would like to make a trial of the wren's egg and the treatment that Albyn had suggested.

For a little while she stood still as the leaves above them in the windless twilight, and then, not looking at Albyn again, not looking at anyone, nodded her head.

'Very well,' said Glam. 'Let us go back to the palace.' And the Oldest Druid made a gesture of despair.

'No,' said Albyn, 'not to the palace. If my treatment is to be effective, my patient must not be disturbed. A more suitable place would be the old stone tower — the broch, you call it — on the shore down there. There is a spring of good water in it, and we shall need enough food to last a fortnight, and the use of a cow. Some sheepskins for comfort, and a load or two of dry wood — '

'There is more comfort in the palace,' said Glam.

'But my patient must not be disturbed,' said Albyn

again. 'I cannot permit even the risk of disturbance.'

'He knows his own mind,' said Furbister to the Oldest Druid, 'which is more than you dare think about.' And when the others moved slowly away — some to the broch, some to the palace to fetch food and firewood — he sat himself down beneath an oak tree, to keep the Druid awake and jeer at his faith.

Under the old round tower, that had been built a hundred years before against invaders from the south, the King stood waiting while his servants from the palace came stumbling down with meal and eggs, with a girdle and a sack of beans, with mead and a quarter of mutton, with a tub of butter and a load of sheepskins, and a cow at the end of a rope. Between the double walls of the broch were little rooms like cells, and a narrow staircase leading to the ramparts. In the centre, open to the sky, a well had been dug, and the massive door in the outer wall was closed by two iron bars, slotted in the stone. Presently, when all had been delivered that Albyn asked for, the door was closed and the King heard the bolts go clattering home.

But still he waited, until above the black tower the moon came up, and in its radiance he saw two figures on the ramparts. Then at last he decided to go home. 'I wish her mother were alive,' he said, and sighing, turned his back upon the moon.

CHAPTER FIVE

'BE still,' said Albyn. 'You must be very careful,
it has so delicate a shell. Try to be calm.'

But now Liss was calmer than he, for the
hardihood with which he had announced a cure for
the Princess, and the confidence with which he had
made the necessary arrangements for it, had not lasted
very long; and now, while Liss waited in tranquillity
for his instructions, Albyn's spirit grew troubled
within him, and his voice when he spoke was hoarse
and unsteady. He remembered the delight and awe,
so strong together that they took his breath away and
made his head swim, when the moon — how long ago?
— had risen behind a fringe of birches on a little hill;
and now again he was moon-dazzled.

He rose from his knees and stumbled to the narrow
window, and looked out upon the sea. It was freckled
with silver light, and a long cloud, like a hill under
winter snow, lay white upon the dark horizon. — To
be so troubled by beauty is the penalty of being a poet,
he thought. In his mind he repeated the phrase, and
complacency, with the lightest of fingers, touched and
comforted him. Had I not been a poet — so his medi-
tation continued — I would not have seen how to
make use of the wren's egg, I could not have brought
her here. So poetry has served me well, for my pain
will go, and she, I hope, will stay. But I must tell her
the truth! I lied to her father, but I must be honest
with her. It will be dangerous, but what else can I do?
This business of the egg — no, honesty's the only

thing. And it's a great relief to be honest, after the first effort has been made.

Moving away from the slit in the wall, he let the moonlight into the room, and Liss on her bed of sheepskins lay as white as the cloud on the horizon. But Albyn did not look at her. He sat on the floor beside her, and with his elbows on his knees and his chin on his hands, said slowly, 'I am no better off than you, for you have lost your voice, and I have lost my wit. An hour ago I was ready to play the philosopher, ready to pretend in a dozen ways that I could cure you. But now I'm as helpless as you. I fell in love with you — at first sight I fell like a roosting pigeon struck by a sling-shot — no! like a hawk stooping, for I wanted, on the instant, to take you down into the heather. So I thought of a trick, a device, to get you to myself, and my vanity said to me that when we were together I could woo you, and make you say *yes* to my pleading. And when you had said *yes*, you would remember other words, I thought. So I told your father a pretty tale about the wren's egg — made up in a moment, for I didn't know she had laid — and now my effort's wasted, and the tale's no use. Furbister silenced you, and you've got your revenge; for you've taken my words from me. I can't talk philosophy, because I don't want to — and I can't woo you either.'

'Why?' asked Liss.

'Because I'm a poet,' said Albyn impatiently, 'and I know when silence is necessary. There are no words for wooing a girl like you. I need new words — words that no one has used before — unsullied words for love, and beauty, and adoration. New words for your arms and your lips, and for your hair. But my mind's

44

distraught — you've disarmed my wit — and I can't find the words that you deserve.'

'Try,' said Liss, as faintly as before.

Albyn turned suddenly, mouth agape in the shadow, and said, 'You're speaking!'

Liss lay smiling, but made no answer.

'You've spoken twice,' he said. 'I hardly noticed the first word — but you spoke, didn't you? Or was it just — '

'A sigh?'

'No, no! You're speaking! Go on, say more. You're cured!'

'It would be so awkward if both of us were dumb,' said Liss.

'I was explaining to you what made me tongue-tied — '

'And naturally I was sympathetic.'

Albyn looked at her suspiciously, and in a voice that was almost fretful said, 'I don't understand what's happened. What cured you?'

'The wren's egg, perhaps.'

'How could it? It was quite an ordinary wren.'

'Are wrens so ordinary? This one laid an egg when it was needed — and it had seen mercy, which is uncommon, and heard gratitude, which is most unusual.'

'I was acting a part when I said that.'

'Were you acting another part when you said that you fell in love with me at first sight?'

'No, that was true. That was heart-spoken, not made by the mind.'

'Perhaps I was condemned to silence till someone should redeem me by speaking truth. Such truth as that.'

'If I say it again, what will you answer?'

'You must teach me,' said Liss. 'I am only learning yet.'

As the moon climbed higher, its light receded from the pile of sheepskins, leaving them in total darkness. For a little while, from the foot of the narrow window-slit, a white radiance lay on the floor in the shape of a long thin slipper; but gradually the light retracted until it shone only on the rough stone sill of the window. Then the sill grew dark, and through the window a glimmering star could be seen.

'The egg!' cried Liss. 'You told me to be careful, and now you've broken it! Oh, Albyn, how clumsy you are!'

CHAPTER SIX

SEVEN days later the rays of the morning sun came in through the window that the moon had lighted, and fell on Albyn's sleeping eyes. He grumbled, rubbed his face, and woke.

Beside him, on their pile of sheepskins, Liss lay dreaming. He turned towards her, leaning on his elbow, and like a pious scholar poring over a page of Ptolemy's seventy scribes, studied yet again the gentle drawing of her lips, the pride of her nostrils, her eyelashes at rest on a rose-leaf skin that was a little darkened by their shadow and half-moist with dew. Letter by letter he spelt her beauty, and twining a lock of hair round his finger, sought comparisons for its colour.

There were single threads that seemed to burn in the sun, but its smooth mass lay like clover honey. Did it smell of honey? Carefully he divided the yellow fleece, and saw her scalp as white as honeycomb. Adoring, he began to count the golden strands that sprang from whiteness, and then the sun, climbing higher, lighted her bare shoulder. — He drew back, and became a mountaineer enthralled by prospect of the snow. To climb that lovely summit! Gently he slid his fingers up her arm, and paused below the curving top, unwilling to intrude upon perfection.

I am in love, he thought. I have loved some forty times already, and before I became a poet I made some forty ballads for my mother. But when I grew into a poet I forgot my ballads, I put them behind me; and now, in the same fashion, I put away my chasing loves. I have found Liss, and life is whole. I want nothing else, but that time should stand still — or pass on, and leave us here.

From contemplation of Liss's shoulder and her golden hair, Albyn turned and lay upon his back to contemplate the rough beams of the ceiling above him, and the exasperating flux of the world that hurried days and months away, good and bad, all at the same mad pace. But in a little while the sunlight, now streaming through the slit in the wall, was cut off; and from the shadow that occluded it a gruff voice spoke.

'So this is how your medicine works!' said Furbister.

'Not so loud!' whispered Albyn, frightened but still thoughtful of his patient. 'Not so loud, or you'll waken her.' — And covering the Princess with a sheepskin he tiptoed to the narrow window, and stared through it, alarmed and angry, at a small section of Furbister's great face and one baleful eye. The giant stood outside, and his head was almost level with the window.

'You're interrupting the cure,' said Albyn.

'I woke early this morning,' said Furbister, muting his voice to a genial growl, 'and I thought I might interrupt something or other if I came to see you. But it was only fair, I decided, to tell you about a new law that I intend to make. A law that says it's treason to lie with the King's daughter. And treason's punishable by death.'

'I've given her back the power of speech that you frightened from her: is that treason?'

'She's talking, is she? Well, that was to be expected, for a silent woman's contrary to nature. — But how did

48

you do it, Albyn? And what's happened to the wren's egg?'

'Be sensible!' implored Albyn. 'You're a man of the world, and so am I — '

'For how long?' asked the giant. 'My new law can separate you from the world by the height of a tree. If I tell the King that I found his daughter and her doctor lying side by side, he'll hang you on the topmost branch in Galloway.'

'But why must you tell him?'

'Because you enjoy your world, and I don't! For the last week I haven't slept two hours a night!'

His voice, growing louder with the rage of his un-happiness, had wakened Liss; who now spoke coldly from her bed, 'If that is Furbister who has come to inquire for me, tell him I am very well.'

'And what shall I tell the King?' shouted the giant.

'That thanks to Albyn, I am completely cured,' said Liss.

'He'll want to know what your medicine was. So will the Druids, and every soul in Galloway!'

Liss, with a sheepskin over her shoulders, another clutched round her waist, got up and walking to the window, pushed Albyn a little to one side. She looked through the slit in the great stone wall and saw, in the shadow of his head, the upper right-hand quarter of the giant's face, and an irately staring eye. Once she had been frightened out of her senses by so near a view, but now she confronted him without a tremor, and in a voice that Albyn had not heard before —the voice of a scold — said, 'Go to my father and tell him the truth: that you came to spy on us!'

'Don't lose your temper,' answered the giant. 'The

truth is that I came as a friend. I came to warn your doctor that I may have to hang him for treason.'

'And who would gain by that?'

'Not Albyn,' said the giant.

'The people would prevent you,' said Liss. 'They are fond of me, and when they know that Albyn has cured me — '

'The people!' exclaimed the giant contemptuously. 'What can they do? You might as well look to a hirsel of sheep.'

Liss grew pale with anger, and Albyn, fearing she would use her new-found tongue to insult the giant beyond forgiveness, hurriedly interposed: 'The real trouble is that Furbister hasn't been sleeping very well, and waking this morning, rather early, he felt lonely—'

'I'm always lonely,' interrupted the giant. 'A man in my position can expect nothing else.'

'I know of a remedy in Northumberland,' said Albyn.

'And you think you can use her to make a bargain with me: is that it?'

'Wasn't that in your mind when you came here?'

Liss, not cold so much as curious now, inquired, 'What are you suggesting?'

'Go and make the breakfast,' said Albyn, 'and I'll tell you later.' Frowning a little, Liss hesitated, and then with a last look of hatred at the giant, obeyed.

'You've got a handful there,' said Furbister when she had gone.

'She's beginning to show a mind of her own,' Albyn admitted. 'It's part of the unexpectedness of love, that it lets a woman put off restraint as well as her clothes. — But you mustn't worry about the girl in Northumberland: I think she's very good-natured.'

'Northumberland's a big country: where does she live?'

'I'm not at liberty to tell you.'

'Well, it doesn't really matter,' said Furbister, 'because I've no intention of going to look for her myself. I can't risk a public refusal: not in my position. But I'll tell you, in confidence, that I've been thinking it over, and I've come to the conclusion that I'd like to see the girl. Now what I suggest is that you go and visit her, with some attendants and a few presents, and invite her to come and stay with me for two or three weeks.'

'It's fifteen or sixteen days' marching — marching light and marching hard — from Wigtown to where she lives. I should be away for more than a month. I'm not going to leave Liss alone for a month or more!'

'If you were convicted of treason, the separation would be longer than that.'

'And if I were hanged, you might have some difficulty in finding the girl — and you'd lose your epic poem as well.'

'It would suit us both,' said Furbister, 'to make a bargain. When can you start?'

'I told the King that the cure would take fourteen days. And I can't promise anything till I've talked to Liss.'

'She'll see reason,' said Furbister. 'It's my experience that royal personages take a very realistic view of life. That's why I've had to get rid of so many. — Well, I won't press the enactment of my new law, Albyn, but I'll make the arrangements for your journey to Northumberland, and I'll see you in a week's time. Goodbye till then.'

Leaning his forehead against the rough masonry of the wall and feeling it cold against his angry skin, Albyn watched the giant, head bent and with long slow strides, walking from the tower; and overcoming a certain hesitancy, he went down to tell Liss the matter of their conversation.

Liss, who had blown up the fire and set the porridge on to boil, was milking the cow with unusual urgency in her wrists and fingers. Albyn told his tale to the accompaniment of hissing and spurting, as the milk frothed into the beechwood tub that she held between her knees; and Liss made no reply until she had stripped the udder of its last drops. Then, giving him the tub to carry indoors, she said with surprising mildness, 'You can't spit to windward, can you?'

'Who taught you that?' asked Albyn, who had never been to sea.

'My uncle,' said Liss. 'He was drowned three years ago. We had a good ship once, that used to trade with Ireland, and he commanded it. He was younger than my father, and I think he might have made a better King. He used to say: "Drive your ship hard, and drive your men hard, so long as the wind's fair and your men are well fed. Learn the way of the tides, be patient in a fog, and never spit to windward." '

'But in spite of his wisdom,' said Albyn, 'he was drowned?'

'Men sail the sea on sufferance. No man can be master of the sea.'

'And Furbister, you mean, is a contrary wind?'

'He won't blow for ever. The greatest giant in history was Galbek, who never stopped growing, and at last he tripped over his own feet and fell into a bog, and was too heavy to pull himself out of it. And the little people, whom he had oppressed, were very thankful and went on living.'

'You think, then, that I ought to go to Northumberland?'

'It will be rather convenient, in some ways,' said Liss, giving him his porridge. 'It'll give me a chance to talk to father, and persuade him to accept you as a son-in-law. It won't be easy, because he's old-fashioned in many ways, and the idea of having a poet in the family isn't going to appeal to him —'

'Why not?' asked Albyn indignantly.

'How could it? You must be reasonable, darling. It's different for me, of course, because I know you. But there's a lot of prejudice against clever people, and on the whole it's justified; because people who are very clever in some particular way, often pay for it by lack of judgment; and so they're quite unreliable in other ways. — But don't worry too much, because if you're away for a month, and father doesn't see you, I'll be able to persuade him that you're not like that at all. I'll tell him you're quite sensible, in fact. — And I'm going to ask him for that field to the north of the town, the one that slopes down to the shore under a curving ridge. I've always thought it was a good place for a house, and while you're away I can get the turf cut, and work started on it.'

'I've never had a house of my own,' said Albyn, 'and I don't think I want one. Won't it be a nuisance?'

'Oh, don't be silly! We must have somewhere to live, and the children will have to have a roof over their heads.'

From the hour of their first breakfast together, it

had surprised Albyn to see so exquisite a creature as Liss — a girl so delicate that when she drank the heather-mead, her throat seemed to darken with its hue — sit down to porridge and eat it with a common hunger; he had learned, however, to accept her appetite as natural, though anomalous. He had discovered that her sensibility, which Furbister had shocked, was not inconsistent with a sturdy mind and a rational attitude. He had become aware, with some foreboding, that her beauty had a hard core. Like the wren, whose egg had been his excuse to woo her, she looked to the eye enchantingly fragile, and yet there was no doubt that she could feed herself and endure the rain. — This calm assumption, however, of her over-ruling womanhood, and its power to control and confine all his life hereafter, roused him to frightened and indignant expostulation. He was a poet, he exclaimed, not a father and a householder. He required freedom to be a poet, and what freedom would there be when he had property to look after and children to rear? Love itself, he declared, could not endure such burdens.

'Poor Furbister can't endure being lonely at night,' said Liss, 'and if you want a wife you must accept what a wife wants. — So finish your porridge and don't be foolish.'

But Albyn had lost his appetite, and leaving her he went into the inner part of the broch, where the little cow stood dreamily twitching its ears, and the round walls, unroofed, enclosed a circle of blue sky. The impregnable tower that he had chosen for his honeymoon looked like a prison now. Even the sky — so much of it as he could see — was shut in by stony ramparts. 'So there are three of us,' he said to the cow, 'a cow, a poet, and the sky itself in jail together. There's no justice in the world!'

He looked at his hands, as though he saw them chained already to a great load of children; and then, from one of the little chambers in the double wall of the broch, he heard Liss singing. He listened for a while, and sighed: 'Who would have thought she had so much determination in her?'

CHAPTER SEVEN

ON the twelfth day of the cure, they had another
visitor. More discreetly than Furbister, the
Oldest Druid came at dusk to inquire for the
Princess, and Albyn, unbarring the door, let him in
and led him to the ramparts; where Liss was watching
the changing light of the sky.

That the Druid was greatly pleased by her recovery
was beyond doubt or question. He was a kindly old
man, and when he heard Liss speaking his eyes filled
with tears. But he was troubled also, and presently in
his gravest voice he said, 'The people have been waiting
most eagerly for news of you, my dear. But though
they have good hearts, they have foolish heads. False
doctrine has always appealed to them more strongly
than the truth — and so it always will, I suppose, or
there can be no virtue in being a priest! — and already
they have seized upon the idea that in a wren's egg
there is some special power of healing. Someone has
invented, and everyone is telling, a tale of contest
between the birds to establish which was king: and
though the eagle, to begin with, soared far above the
rest, the prize was taken by a wren that had had the
foresight to conceal itself in the eagle's feathers till
the eagle was exhausted. That foolish tale is now
common property, and attendance at our services has
fallen off because half the people are wandering about
the fields, to stop and listen whenever they hear a bird
singing, *Titty-titty-titty-tick*. Every little boy, moreover,
is robbing the nests of hedge-sparrows, chaffinches,

thrushes, blackbirds and larks, and old women who ought to know better are using their eggs to doctor boils and burns, toothache and life-long cripples, and women in labour. — So neither of you, I hope, will say anything to suggest that your cure was obtained by magic, for we all know that any good thing in the world is the work of God alone.'

Albyn and Liss both assured him that, in their opinion, the wren's egg had been of no material importance in her recovery; and the Oldest Druid was much relieved to hear it. He spoke again about the dangers of superstition, and gave them some local gossip. So-and-so's cow had dropped twin calves, both doing well; a goose in a neighbouring village had in old age turned into a gander; Furbister had been in a most tyrannical temper, and was threatening to send an expedition against a small, half-nomadic tribe that lived in the debatable land between Galloway and Carrick — and this, the Druid thought, would be an injudicious move.

So, pleasantly enough, they passed an hour or two, and when the old man had gone and Albyn had barred the door behind him, Liss said: 'Now we have less need to worry. It would have been very awkward to describe your treatment — darling, I do hope you'll be my doctor for ever and ever! — but now the Druids will save us from any embarrassment by taking full responsibility for everything that's happened. They'll tell the people to praise God, and make it quite clear that if it hadn't been for them, God wouldn't have moved a finger. I'll have to make a speech, and every word I say will be quoted as testimony to the power of priesthood. Just you see!'

'I think I ought to get some credit,' said Albyn.

'You've got me,' said Liss. 'Isn't that enough?'

'But in justice,' said Albyn, 'I deserve recognition for what I've done.'

'Oh, my dear, how innocent you are! You may be a poet, but you know almost nothing about life. — Don't you realize that wherever there's an official priesthood, the priests must take the credit if anything happens that the mass of people desire to happen? Don't you know that Furbister has to be praised for every battle we win, though the real fighting may have been done by some quite unknown person from Palnackie or Auchencairn? Have you never seen a woman being congratulated on the birth of a man-child, a great, red-faced, howling infant, the very image of its father — but no one ever says a word about his part in the business?'

'And do you think that's fair?'

'It's reasonably fair,' said Liss. 'The father had had his pleasure in the begetting of the child. The soldier from Palnackie or Auchencairn had already been rewarded by Furbister because Furbister wanted to retain his loyalty. And you've had the agreeable experience of living with me for a whole fortnight, without having to explain to my father how we occupied our time. — Life isn't ideal, it never will be, and perfect justice doesn't exist. But life is full of compensation, and the sensible person who doesn't expect too much can get a lot of enjoyment out of it.'

'If I'd been as easily satisfied as that,' said Albyn, 'I wouldn't be here tonight. I've always wanted perfection, I've never been satisfied with less — and that's why we're lying under the same sheepskin.'

'What a pretty excuse for improper behaviour!'

'Are you vain?'

'How can I be, if I'm perfect?'

'Perfection's entitled to a looking-glass.'

'I must be vain: I like flattery more.'

The sensation of capture and imprisonment, by which Albyn had been oppressed when he first perceived the practical side of Liss's nature, had not lasted long; and their two remaining days in the broch were spent in such lively bliss that when at last they had to leave it — for the Druids and the King and all the population of Wigtown were waiting for them — he felt, not release, but as though he were being expelled from a paradise that he would never re-enter; and Liss, clinging to his hand, was grave as he, and a little tearful.

As soon as they came out of the broch, the Druids took charge of them. The King was allowed to greet his daughter, and hear her voice, but as soon as they had exchanged a score of words, the Druids raised a triumphal hymn, a procession was formed and they all marched to the Oak Trees for the service of thanksgiving.

Under the Oak Trees no mention was made of Albyn's remedy, and later, at the palace, the King was so entranced by his daughter's voice that he could not hear enough of it. He showed, inexplicably, no desire for conversation with the poet who had cured her. With the utmost courtesy he expressed his gratitude, but he gave Albyn no chance to talk about himself, his philosophy, his past, or his future. Nor could Albyn find occasion to speak with Liss, but had to spend two of the weariest hours of his life in meaningless talk with members of the household, and elderly women who insisted on telling him about their own experiments with medicine. — He remembered what Liss had said, and tried to persuade himself that it was better to be altogether ignored than questioned too closely; but he felt, none the less, that he was entitled to more attention than he had received.

It was, then, almost with pleasure that he received a message from Furbister. One of the giant's people approached him, very civilly, to say that Furbister wished to speak to him; and would he be so kind as to come to the other palace? Albyn saw no reason why he should not leave the company in which he was neglected, and followed the messenger at once.

He found Furbister in his lofty hall with some eight or ten of his household, and as many townsfolk, to whom he was giving instructions for the reception of his Northumbrian visitor. He wanted a couple of chairs made, almost as big as the enormous one in which he sat. His palace must be enlarged: they would have to fell trees, cut turf, to build another room, and build it high. Blankets must be woven, six ells long and four broad. — His forehead was deeply wrinkled, his thought so concentrated on preparations for his guest, that for a few minutes he failed to notice Albyn. But when at last he saw him, his welcome was warm, he called for mead, and at once began to talk about Albyn's journey to Northumberland. All the arrangements had been made, said Furbister, and he described them in detail.

No more than in the King's palace was Albyn given a chance to speak about himself, and his hopes. The giant showed not the slightest interest in his affairs, but talked unceasingly of the Northumbrian girl, and the presents he was sending her, and the chairs he was designing for her comfort. The townsfolk and the members of his household stood round him, listening obediently, and Albyn dutifully agreed that some sheepskins, which had been dyed scarlet, would be acceptable gifts. He drank as much mead as was given him, and grew more and more depressed. He wanted only to go back to Liss, but when Furbister had finally exhausted the topic of his visitor and her journey, he yawned once or twice — opening a mouth like a small sea-cave — and said, 'It's getting late. You'd better put a rug down beside the fire, and make yourself comfortable.'

'Here?' exclaimed Albyn.

'I told the King that I'd take care of you. You'll have to make an early start tomorrow.'

He looked at Albyn maliciously now, grinning at his dismay, and said: 'You won't be as comfortable as you've lately been, but turn-about's fair play. It's time to think of my pleasure now.'

He got up, laughing, and went off to his own chamber. As soon as he had gone, about forty men-at-arms came in, talking noisily; and roughly pulling benches away from the wall, spread each his plaid and blanket in the place where he was accustomed to sleep. For at night the great hall became a dormitory, and Albyn, thrust far away from the fire, lay among the soldiers — some talking loudly still, some snoring — and realized that great happiness has its disadvantages.

A few weeks ago, he thought, I should have slept as soundly as this brute beside me; for the truth is that I am comfortable enough except for my memory of how much more comfortable I was last night. To be happy makes the mind so tender that it cannot bear the loss of happiness. — But was I never happy until I met Liss? I must have been; and took it so lightly that I can't remember now. There's much to be said for living lightly and caring little; but to fall in love's like picking blackberries naked: the fruit's out of reach, and there's a host of thorns. If Liss doesn't come in the morning, if I don't see her before I go . . .

He rolled over on his blanket and lay face to the ground, his head on his fore-arms, as if to turn his back on this new fear. And presently a traitorous thought entered his mind: he was a poet — he had almost forgotten it — and for a poet unhappiness was valuable. It would give him the darker hues he must weave into his verse, when the time came for composition. Dark hues were highly regarded. They proceeded from a certain richness of the spirit, and this richness he was now acquiring. — Poor Liss, he thought, had no such comfort. She too, being lonely, might be unhappy; and unhappiness would do her no good. It was a blessed thing to be a poet.

Soon he was fast asleep, and waking in the morning, amid a surly clamour, he got a horn of ale and a round of oat-bread to break his fast. In a little while he heard Furbister shouting for him, and going out saw the giant standing with a group of men and a train of ponies. He was to have an escort of six, and there were four pack-ponies loaded with presents for the young giantess.

Furbister was in a loud and genial mood, making unwieldy jokes, but impatient for them to be off. There was a little crowd of idlers to watch their start, and

Albyn looked anxiously to see if Liss was there, or any of her women. He saw no one whom he knew, but while Furbister was exhorting the leader of the escort to make all haste, another man whispered to him, 'The Princess is waiting for you beyond the river.' — For in those days the town lay south of it.

Albyn mounted in a hurry, and cried, 'Let's be off! Good-bye, Furbister. It'll be your turn next month — and mine too, I hope.'

The giant shouted a farewell, but Albyn, paying no attention, led his troop out of town at a canter, pack-ponies and all. When they approached the river, however, he let the others go ahead, more slowly now, while he lingered behind them. He crossed the ford, and half a mile beyond it saw Liss come out of a road-side cottage.

'How lonely I was last night!' he said, and dismounted beside her.

'I got up before dawn to meet you here,' she said. 'Are you angry with my father?'

'He showed no interest in me, and I'm not much attracted to him.'

'But you're not angry? You'll come back, won't you?'

'As quickly as I can.'

'Oh, my dear! I was afraid we had offended you, and I should never see you again!'

'How foolish you are. And a few days ago I thought how wise you were.'

'You can't be wise when you're afraid. Men often do go away and don't come back.'

'I'm deeper in love than you think, and I can't climb out as easily as you suppose.'

'I told my father that you loved me. It was after that he refused to talk to you, and kept me away from you.'

'Does he know the other side of it: that you love me?'

'He will when you come back. I've a whole month to tell him, a month to persuade him that I know my own mind and must have my own way.'

'Come with me to Northumberland.'

'I'll walk a mile with you, but no more.'

'Who lives in this cottage?'

'A woman who used to be my nurse. I'll come back and have my dinner here.'

'I'll stay till dinner-time.'

Liss looked at him, irresolute, and Albyn hobbled his pony and let it graze. By noon, however, she was self-controlled and practical again — a little sharp, indeed — and told him firmly that he must go.

CHAPTER EIGHT

A FEW miles from Rothbury there lived a worthy
man called Harfa, and his wife, Rhu, who were
the pity of the countryside. The neighbours, in
the English habit of the time, did what they could to
lighten their burden by pretending that it did not
exist; or, when confronted with it, by behaving as
though there was nothing extraordinary about it. But
in their own homes they would shake their heads,
saying that Harfa would be a ruined man before next
harvest; and pray that no giant or giantess should ever
be born in their beds.

Harfa, when he married, had been the wealthiest
man in the district, and his wife had brought him a
good property that added to his riches. But their
daughter, Bala, now eighteen years old and four hands
above the two-fathom mark, had eaten all the produce
of their farms, all they could breed and grow, and for
many years Harfa had taken nothing to market, for
when her appetite was satisfied there was nothing left.

They were fond of their daughter, after a fashion,
and if she only had been of normal size they would
have had as much reason for affection as most parents.
Bala was not ill-looking. Her enormous figure was
well-proportioned, her features undistinguished but
inoffensive except for narrow eyes that gave her a look
of slyness. She was tolerably good-humoured, fond of
animals — many of which she killed in the strength of
her caresses — and had she been given her own way,
would have been high-spirited. Her humour, however,

was so destructive that it had to be repressed. A hundred times at least Rhu had said to her husband, 'If she was a quarter the size, I wouldn't wish for a better daughter. But, oh, Harfa, what are we going to do with her?' — And Harfa would sit glumly in his chair, and wonder why they had been doomed to carry such a burden.

Only Ferli loved the young giantess without afterthought or reservation. Ferli was a year younger than Bala, a niece of Rhu's, and an orphan. Harfa and Rhu had adopted her, and she had repaid them handsomely by her devotion to their daughter. She was a dark-haired, nimble girl, with blue eyes and black lashes, and a laughing mouth. She was nearly a beauty, but her nose was made for easy breathing rather than admiration, and a mole on the outskirts of her chin did her no service. It was Ferli who brought the news that there were strangers in the valley.

She and Bala had seen them — half a dozen mounted men or more, with pack-horses as well — and Bala had hidden in the wood, as she always did when strangers came near. The horsemen had gone to the village, a mile away, but now two of them were coming up the farm-road.

Harfa went out to meet them, and saw that one was a servant, leading two laden ponies. He did not recognize the other until Albyn had taken his hand and told him his name. Albyn, who had grown up in the years since their last meeting, thought that Harfa had aged more than that. He told his man to unload and hobble the ponies, and followed his host indoors.

Ferli, who sat with them — listening closely and never taking her eyes off Albyn — cried out in shrill excitement when she heard the purpose of his visit; but Harfa and Rhu stared at him with a deeper emotion in their eyes, and Rhu took her husband's hand in hers and pressed it tightly.

'Will I go and fetch Bala?' demanded Ferli.

'She will have to decide for herself,' said Rhu doubtfully. Ferli ran off at once.

'Tell us more about Furbister,' said Harfa, and Albyn made a good story of the giant's power in Scotland, without saying much about his less amiable qualities. He could see clearly enough that neither Harfa nor Rhu wanted any ground or pretext for refusing Furbister's offer, and he was careful to give them none. He told them instead of the mild weather they had on the coast of Galloway.

Then in the distance they heard Bala's voice. Quickly it grew louder — for she was running, and calling over her shoulder to Ferli, who had been left behind — and when she reached the house, and saw Furbister's presents spread out before the door, she exclaimed in such vociferous delight that Albyn was reminded of a snow-field, thaw-loosened, falling over a cliff in spring. He went out with her parents and saw her standing, in enormous rapture, before a pile of scarlet sheepskins, an array of ornaments and jewellery made of sea-shells, a string of mussel-pearls in a black box, half a dozen cheeses, and a haunch of salt venison — for Furbister knew well the pangs of hunger that torment a giant. Bala, now cooing like a stream in spate, now uttering trills of delighted laughter like hammers pounding in a smithy, stood bent above this various array; and Albyn, though well used to Furbister's huge bulk, was daunted by the scale of her womanhood and its enormous opulence. While he stood marvelling, he heard Ferli's voice, a little breathless, at his shoulder.

'Isn't she happy?' said Ferli. 'I've always wanted to see her like this.'

'Why?' asked Albyn.

'It's what she needs.'

Before he could reply, Bala demanded of her parents, 'Is Furbister as big as I am?'

'You must ask Albyn,' said Harfa.

Bala had not noticed him before, but now, bending so suddenly that it seemed the sky grew dark and a pair of moons came plunging from it, she cried, 'How tall is my sweetheart?'

'About four hands higher than you.'

'How wonderful he must be! When shall we start?'

'You're quite sure that you want to marry him?' asked Rhu.

'Of course!' shouted Bala.

'Dear Bala!' whispered Ferli, close to Albyn's shoulder. 'She will make a splendid wife!'

They went into the tall building, like a barn, that had been built beside the farmhouse for Bala's accommodation, and Albyn again described her gigantic wooer and his dominions. Bala sat with one of the red sheepskins on her lap, and played with her new jewellery. Her knees, bared by the lifting of her frock, were like boulders in a mountain stream, but her expression was childishly complacent, though a little sly. From time to time she asked sensible questions. 'What does Furbister have for his dinner?' she inquired.

Her parents, hopeful but anxious, looked very old

and small beside her, but remembered their responsibilities.

'There's a priesthood in your country?' asked Rhu. 'She'll be properly married?'

'I'm sure she will,' said Albyn. 'The Druids have a lot of influence, and the King is one of the old-fashioned sort.'

'Isn't Furbister the King?' asked Bala in surprise.

'No, the King's name is Glam.'

'Is he bigger than Furbister?'

'He's about the same height as your father.'

'Then why doesn't Furbister get rid of him?'

Albyn discussed the advantages of an hereditary monarchy, shrewdly enough, but without convincing Bala; and when he left them, to return to the village, it occurred to him that, in spite of her youth and apparent simplicity, she might be ambitious.

In the morning he sent a man with the remaining pack-ponies, and the rest of Furbister's presents, to the farm; but he himself stayed in the village. He had met a man he knew, a runaway from the Roman armies in the south of England, with whom he had talked some half a dozen years before; and now this man, Onesimus by name — though no one in the village could pronounce it — had five friends with him, deserters from the service too. Onesimus had married a Northumbrian woman, a widow with a little property of her own, and he was looking after the others till they could find occupation or wives for themselves. Onesimus had acquired status and a pot-belly in his new home; the others, still unsure of themselves, looked always for his approval when they spoke.

One came from Gaul, one from Spain, two were

natives of Calabria, Onesimus had been born in Thessaly, and the sixth in Syria: they all disliked the discipline of Rome, and had escaped from it. Their tales of army life were monotonous, but Albyn found much to interest him when they spoke of their own countries, of the faith and customs of their own people. None of them knew why the Romans had invaded England, though the Spaniard believed it was to secure the oyster-beds that lay off the coast of Essex, and one of the Calabrians was sure that it was merely a device to swindle the soldiers of their pay. They all agreed that since landing in England they had been paid very irregularly.

Harfa sent word that Bala was ready and eager to start on her journey, but Albyn replied that he was going to spend another day in the village. He wanted to hear more about the Roman service, and far parts of the world, and the deserters were willing enough to tell him all they knew. The Northumbrians never listened to them, for though they were not averse to foreigners, they were quite uninterested in foreign affairs. — But Albyn sat for two days, and kept the soldiers talking. They told him that the Romans were masters of all the south-eastern corner of England. 'But they'll find it harder to advance north or west-ward,' said Onesimus, with the complacent pessimism of the old soldier; and all the others agreed. Five of them had run away after the bitter campaign to put down the Icenian revolt — 'None of us wanted any more soldiering after that,' said the Spaniard — but Onesimus had escaped before there was any threat of revolt, and was proud of his foresight in having taken so early a decision.

They sat late into the night, and Albyn was a little

taciturn when, in the morning, he set out on his west-ward journey. The ponies that had carried Furbister's presents were now laden with Bala's goods, and Ferli rode with them to attend her. Harfa and Rhu took farewell of their daughter with a very decent show of grief, but both of them, thought Albyn, already looked ten years younger. Bala made no concealment of her impatience to be off, and he had some difficulty in restraining her from leading his troop at a pace the ponies could not match. 'She's full of life,' said Ferli, riding beside him.

They rode north and to the west, and crossing the Coquet at Alwinton, climbed the bare hills to drop again to the banks of the Rede, and so into Scotland at Carter Fell. Then there was more climbing, and steep descents, till they came into Liddisdale and rode down to the trees and Bala's first sight of the sea. But she paid no attention to salt water, beyond sniffing a little at the smell of the ebb, until in a village near Annan she was given a score of small flounders, well fried, for her supper; and after that she took a kindlier interest in it. Her mind was full of her approaching marriage, and during most of their march she was far in front and fretful when she had to wait for the tired ponies to catch her up.

For the first two or three days Ferli rode with her, or close behind; but then, more often, with Albyn. She was a talkative girl, and again and again she told him how warm-hearted Bala was, but how lonely she had been because of her great size. 'She used to hide when strangers came, but look at her now! She doesn't care who sees her. Oh, it's doing her good already, to know that she's appreciated.'

Bala, indeed, was quite indifferent to the staring curiosity of the people they met, and the villages through which they passed; and once, when a lively sailor in a small sea-port shouted to his mate, 'She'd keep us warm at night, wouldn't she?' — Bala shouted back, 'I'm going to warm a better man than you, little fellow!' And for an hour thereafter, greatly pleased with her quick reply, she laughed aloud as she marched.

Ferli laughed too, sharing the joke with Albyn. They talked easily together, riding side by side, and the soldiers of the escort, to whom Ferli paid no attention, made jealous comments on their friendship. Ferli's manner had become engaging enough — sometimes a little provocative, a little warmly flustered — to excite their interest; but Albyn saw none of her charms and heard nothing of the sentiment in her voice, for he, to see Liss again, was almost as impatient as Bala to meet her giant. He was more reasonable than Bala, however: he would not let the ponies be ridden to exhaustion, and he could talk of other things than that to which he most looked forward.

It was not until they drew near Kirkcudbright that he said anything of Liss, and he was astonished at the consequence of what he said. — Ferli had been talking of Bala's wedding, and Albyn, for courtesy's sake, to keep conversation going when it appeared to flag, said that he also looked forward to being married soon after their arrival. — Ferli turned pale, cried, 'Why did you not tell me before?'

'I didn't suppose it would interest you,' said Albyn.

'Oh, nonsense. What nonsense! Everybody's interested in people who're going to get married. It was hateful of you not to tell me before!' — And

72

to his immense surprise she whipped up her pony, and galloped in pursuit of Bala; who, as usual, was half a mile ahead.

Albyn, deeply puzzled, looked at her crouching over her pony's neck, and the dust rising behind them; then shrugged his shoulders. The day was hot, and girls, he knew, were unstable creatures. He turned and beckoned to the leader of his escort, and calculated with him that they could expect to complete their double journey in thirty-one days. They had been fortunate, they agreed. Two or three days had been wasted, perhaps, where they were uncertain of the road, but nowhere had their passage been hindered; nowhere had they met hostility.

'Furbister's talking nonsense,' said Albyn, 'when he pretends that the clans beyond the Nith, in Annandale and about the Esk, are a danger to peace.'

'To a man in his position,' said the leader of the escort, 'it isn't things as they are that are important. It's just his own ideas about them that he considers.— I'm saying nothing against Furbister, mind you! He pays us well, and I've got hopes of promotion. But I don't believe what he says, and never have done.'

'Poor Galloway,' said Albyn. 'And poor Furbister!'

'He's all right,' said the soldier, 'so long as Bala isn't too much for him.'

Furbister, striding all alone, met them at Creetown. Bala, more impatient than usual, had been a full mile ahead of the troop, and came running back, in preposterous tumult, to say there was a man on the road. 'A man!' she cried. 'The biggest man in the world. I'm frightened!'

Albyn rode on, and met Furbister, sweating and out of breath.

'Was that her?' he demanded. 'That glorious being? Where is she?'

'There,' said Albyn, 'hiding behind the peat-stack.'

The peat-stack, though newly built to supply a prosperous farm with all its winter fuel, was no covert for Bala; two enormous feet, their leathery soles all white with dust, and calves as red and sturdy as pine trees, protruded from one end of it. Furbister, snorting like a stone-horse, strode forward — purposeful and majestic — and exclaimed, 'My love! My bride!'

Bala, with a joyful scream, took to her heels and pelted for the hills. Blindly she ran through a duck pond. Mud and water rose in a double fountain, expelled by the huge impact of her feet, and ducks fled squawking with terror. Furbister, for a moment or two, stood entranced by her strapping agility; and then, bellowing with delight, pursued her.

'I think,' said Albyn, 'we should ride on to Wigtown.'

'Can I come with you?' asked Ferli in a tremulous voice.

'Of course,' said Albyn, and clapped her on the shoulder.

They met the people of Wigtown long before they reached the town itself; for all its inhabitants had come out, in pursuit of Furbister, to see him meet his bride. But Albyn and his escort, with Ferli beside him, rode clattering through their midst, ignoring their shrill or hoarse inquiries, until they came to the King's palace. There they dismounted, and Albyn, taking Ferli by the hand, went into the great hall.

At the far end of it, in their stately chairs, sat the King and his daughter with the chief Druids and a score or so of elderly attendants on either side. The shadowed hall seemed curiously still, and those who waited there had a withdrawn and slightly anxious look, as though they had taken refuge from the hurly-burly outside. The King had been dozing, and woke with a little start as Albyn, with Ferli holding his hand, came to a halt before him.

'I have done what I was sent to do,' said Albyn. 'I have brought home a bride for Furbister.'

'She's very small,' said the King.

'This is Ferli, her friend from childhood. Furbister's bride, when I last saw her, was running into the hills — but not as fast as she might have been — with Furbister close behind her.'

'Surely it would have been more courteous,' said the King, 'if she had come to see me first.'

He looked from side to side, to Liss and to his councillors, and though he rarely troubled to be angry it was evident that he was displeased. Before he could speak, however, the Oldest Druid came forward and said, 'The wolf and the grasshopper share God's bounty, Your Majesty, and unlikely though it seems, it may be that He has granted even Furbister some little season of happiness. If that be so, let those of us who enjoy Him diuturnally be complaisant towards what can only be a transitory and a fractional dispensation of His mercy.'

A little puzzled by the Druid's conjecture of a mathematical Deity, the King thought for a moment or two, and then said very reasonably, 'Well, there's nothing I can do about it, is there?'

'Albyn,' said the Druid, 'has fulfilled what we are bound to regard as a duty to the Kingdom.'

'I'm well aware of that, and I was just going to thank him. — We're grateful to you, most grateful. It can't have been a very pleasant task, and you were commendably quick about it. Did you have a good journey?'

'The roads were bad, but wherever we went the people were friendly.'

'Tell Furbister that. He won't believe you, but tell him all the same.'

The King rose and left the hall. A few of his councillors followed him, and Liss came to speak to Ferli. They talked for half an hour together, walking in the hall, while Albyn waited. Then Liss called one of her women and said, 'Let her sleep in my chamber. — I'm going back to the broch tonight,' she explained to Albyn. 'I always slept so well during my cure. I think the air is better there.'

CHAPTER NINE

HER father, said Liss, had refused outright to accept a poet as his son-in-law. He couldn't get on with clever people, he had explained. He didn't like them, and he didn't believe in them.

Day after day she had argued with him, but though he listened to all she had to say, he would not change his mind. He himself, he declared, had never been much of a scholar, or sharp and glib with words, but he had always ruled his people in a decent and acceptable way till Furbister came along. Furbister brought new ideas about government, and because he had been able to impose them by brute force, he was ruining the country. 'It isn't his appetite that's the curse of Galloway,' the King had said, 'it's his ideas. He's a gross fellow, but we could put up with that; the unforgivable thing is that he's clever too. He thinks for himself — and only for himself — and if I weren't here to hinder him, he might think more. I can't hinder him much, but once or twice I've worried him and prevented, I dare say, a bit more folly.'

'Another day,' Liss went on, 'he said to me: "I'm an ordinary man, and my kingdom's full of ordinary people. Every kingdom is. But when you've lived with them for a long time, you know that ordinary people are extraordinarily different. Your clever fellows, however, don't see that. They think they're all the same. Because clever fellows are so taken up with their own ideas that they can't be bothered looking at ordinary people, and therefore know very little about them. And that's why I won't have a clever man in my own family.'"

'In some ways,' said Albyn, 'I'm not very clever.'

'I told him that,' said Liss. 'But he said you had talked very glibly about the wren's egg, and it was talk of that sort that he particularly disliked. It was right and proper for a blacksmith to be clever with his hammer, he said, because otherwise he would only be wasting good iron. But a clever tongue didn't make horse-shoes; it only confused people.'

'We shall have to run away,' said Albyn.

'Indeed we shan't!' said Liss. 'You don't suppose I was taken in by all that nonsense? Or was going to submit to it? — No, indeed! I went to see the Oldest Druid and reminded him of what you had done for him and his priesthood by not claiming that you had used magic to cure me. You can always rely on the Druids to be fair: if you do anything for them, they'll remember it and be grateful. The Oldest Druid wasn't difficult at all. He only asked me if I was sure that I knew my own mind, and would promise to bring the children to the Oak Trees at the proper times —'

'Don't talk as if we're going to have a whole troop of them!'

'I must have something to interest me after you've ceased to. — Don't interrupt: that won't be a for a long time yet. — Well, then the Druid said he would speak to father, and I really think he enjoyed having a chance to bully him.'

'Was he successful?'

'I think — I'm not quite sure — but I think he rebuked father for spiritual pride. Anyway, whatever he said was effective and we can be married as soon as the house is ready.'

'Is it really necessary to have a house? A house is very like a trap.'

'Are you afraid of getting caught, as if you were a fox or an otter?'

'Otters do get caught.'

'Yes, and that's something you could talk about to father. You must learn to talk to him, and if you avoid general ideas and just speak about practical things, I dare say you'll get on very well together. — About otters, for example. Father likes otters. He thinks they're far more destructive to eels than to salmon, and you might suggest that one way of preserving them would be to put a tax on their skins. — Then there's rheumatism: do you know a good cure for it?'

'There isn't one.'

'Well, you ought to think of something — buttermilk wouldn't do any harm — because our head shepherd is quite crippled with it, and father's very fond of him and would be pleased if you took an interest in his case. And there's always farming, of course: do you know much about it?'

'I like sitting under a haycock in the sun.'

'That's not very helpful. — Couldn't you tell him that heavy clay's improved by spreading seaweed on it? There was a sailor from the Outer Isles who told us about that, and some people in the Rhinns have been trying it. And say that small farmers ought to be encouraged, because they keep the bracken down, while the big graziers neglect their pasture, though they pay a better rent for it. — Don't talk about sea-shells, unless you're interested, because he's a bore about them. But he's quite sensible about bees.'

'I like the sort of honey that's the colour of your hair.'

'Haven't you any practical knowledge? Have you never done any work?'

'Of course not. I'm a poet.'

'I've never heard any of your poetry.'

'No one has.'

'Haven't you made any?'

'Not yet.'

'Are you going to?'

'I think it might be a waste of time. *Being* is so much more important than *doing*.'

'That,' said Liss, 'is the sort of remark my father would detest!'

CHAPTER TEN

THE Oldest Druid was happier than he had
been for many years. Sitting under the Oak
Trees, with an expression of the utmost benignity on his sere and wrinkled face, he was meditating
the address in which, with a ferocious emphasis on his
unique and absolute power to do so, he would invoke
God's blessing on the marriage of Furbister and Bala.
He would make the giant wince — so he promised
himself — and his great bride should quail.

He had been grimly prepared for Furbister's refusal
of his priestly office, and he was almost childishly delighted when Albyn told him that Bala had been
brought up with a due regard for the spiritual powers,
and that her mother had insisted on a nuptial ceremony
of the proper sort. He went to see the young giantess,
and though he could not find in her either the humility
that he hoped for, or the reverence to which he was
entitled, she had the conventional view of what a wedding should be. And Furbister, patting with ponderous
fingers her massive hand, had fondly agreed to do
whatever she wished.

Before they could be married, however, Wigtown
had to be rebuilt. Its streets were too narrow for
Furbister and Bala to walk down them side by side,
and this, she declared, they must frequently do. It was
incumbent on her, she thought, to take an interest in
the townsfolk, and she wanted to show off her new-
found happiness. It was decided, therefore, to abandon

the old town and build a new one on a more spacious site to the north of the river.

As all the houses were built of turf and timber, and rarely lasted for more than eight or ten years in any case, this was by no means an impossible undertaking, but the people of Wigtown, who had to neglect all their own affairs, found the labour irksome; and some were quick to say that Furbister's marriage would bring nothing but trouble to their country. They were mistaken, however, and within a year or so had forgotten all their forebodings.

Liss had already built her house, in the field by the shore, and the King refused to leave his palace. A few of his councillors, and some others, chose also to remain in the old town, which now shrank to the likeness of a small untidy village clustered about one great house. As all the timber, however, had been removed from the deserted buildings, to be used in the new town, they soon collapsed into little mounds and hillocks of green turf; and in a year's time there were sheep and cattle grazing where a numerous people had lived.

The streets in the new town — there were two of them — were broad enough for Furbister and Bala to walk arm-in-arm down the middle, and their palace was even larger than Furbister's former residence. The Druids declared that the seventh day of the next new moon would promise happiness for their marriage, and Furbister's men scattered far and wide through the country to levy a large tribute of sheep and cattle, meal and ale and salt fish, for a great feast that would last three days. Everywhere there was vast excitement except in the remnants of the old town, where the King and his household never spoke of the approaching ceremony except to say, in self-congratulation, that they would at least be spared the noise of it; while Albyn and Liss, now married for a month or more, were usually too intent on their own affairs to think much of Furbister and his.

The King, who had taken a great dislike to Bala — though she had behaved fairly well when she was presented — had to keep to his bed with lumbago on the wedding-day; but Liss and Albyn were present at the service, though they had quarrelled the day before. — Albyn, having told again the story of his journey to Rothbury, and his return with Bala, had begun to laugh. To begin with he laughed moderately enough, like any decent man when he is tickled by a good joke, but in a little while his laughter grew deeper and louder, until his whole body was shaken by it, as if the fingers of some inexpressible drollery were groping and tickling the soles of his feet and the tenderness under his ribs and the risible parts below his arms. His face grew red, his eyes shed tears, his mouth gaped foolishly, and when he had breath for it he still cried, 'Ho, ho, hoh!' — Liss, curious to begin with, and laughing a little too, though she did not know why, grew impatient at last; and taking him by the shoulders, shook him and demanded to be told the joke.

'Bala,' said Albyn, panting and wiping his eyes. 'Furbister too, but Bala still more.'

'She is gross and stupid, vain and ridiculous,' said Liss. 'I don't find her laughable at all. I find her disgusting. And Furbister — '

'Yes, you've reason to hate him; but you're wrong about both of them. They may offend your eyes, they may displease your nose, they may torment your ear —

but if your mind is whole enough and sturdy enough, they should tickle and regale your mind, and make you fall on your back and laugh!'

'They make me ashamed.'

'But why? They're not the same as you! They're monsters! — You've got a nose, and so has Old Urna the tanner: but Urna's nose hangs down like a pig's ear, like a cod's tail in the fish-wife's hand, like a carrot with the rain-drops dripping from the bulb — and all the children laugh at it because they know what's wrong with it. It's too big! There's Rata the beggar, a kind and decent creature, but every stranger who sees her bursts out laughing because her feet are the size of a young halibut. Nobody laughs at your feet — though anyone's foot, if you try to look at it for the first time, is only a joke to keep an animal upright — but nobody laughs at your feet, because they're the proper size. It's a bigness beyond nature, three times too big, that strangers see in Rata's feet; and that's what makes them laugh! And the Oldest Druid — he's a sensible man and a good man in many ways — but who hasn't derided him when he pretends to speak with all the knowledge and the potency of God? Anything that grows too big is a joke! Whatever swells, or sprouts, or assumes too much is ludicrous. For children, and the poor, and little things we're sorry; little things are pathetic. But at giants, and rich men bloated by their wealth, and things that have grown big beyond proportion, we want to laugh, and we're right to laugh. I'm fond of Furbister, but I think he's a joke. I'm not very fond of Bala, and I'm sure she's a joke.'

'Furbister has been the death of hundreds of people

in Galloway. Bala may be the death of hundreds more.'

'If you think about Furbister's victims, you'll feel sad; but when you think about Furbister — and still more about Bala — you ought to laugh!'

'That's callous! You can't separate the doer from the deed.'

'When a fisherman goes out to fish, do you make no distinction between him and the haddock he catches?'

'That's not the same thing at all — '

'It's a very good parallel.'

'I don't agree.'

'That merely shows your lack of understanding.'

'Do you suggest that if I don't accept your view — '

'I suggest, in that case, that you refuse to recognize facts . . .'

There was the beginning of their quarrel; and when morning came both were unhappy and each was still perplexed by the other's stupidity. But at the proper time they set out for the Oak Trees with an air of high decorum, and after exchanging polite or friendly salutations with a great number of people whom they met on the way, they joined a few friends on a little knoll to the right of the Tree under which the Oldest Druid would stand; and watched the gathering crowd.

From many miles around the people came, a great show of colour in their green and yellow plaids, and filled all the space in front of the Trees but for roads left open for the giant and his bride. Then at noon, Furbister and Bala, with a portentous slowness, approached from opposite directions. They wore long white wedding gowns — Bala's head was hooded — and behind each of them came a little train of attendants, like the wavering tail of a kite. When they reached the Oldest Tree they turned and faced it, side by side, and the priests began to sing the nuptial hymn. Still and solemn and enormous stood the two giants, and all the people, singing lustily but out of tune, looked up at them with necks astrain and gaping mouths. Despite the tyranny under which they lived, they were moved by common experience and the universal impulse to a genuine sympathy with Furbister and Bala; for most of them were married, and the marriage service recalled their generous youth. Goodwill suffused them — and in its sentimental light their faces, thought Albyn, looked like a heap of apples laid by for winter. Innocent, russet-red and sweet, but somewhat tasteless — and the wasps had got at them, that was why they gaped.

The Oldest Druid came out from the shadow of the grove, and in an impressive voice addressed the bridal couple. Unfortunately, however, he stood too near them, and quickly perceived that he was speaking to the white curtain of their gowns, a little above the level of their knees. He tilted his chin, to look higher, but could see only the gathered linen that covered certain flexures and rotundities — Furbister was growing a little paunchy, and Bala had been eating nobly at his table — so pausing in his discourse, and stepping back a pace or two, he looked up again. But still white vestures met his gaze — a tableland and rolling hills of white — for Furbister was massively built, and Bala endowed more richly still. Back again stepped the Druid, stumbling over an exposed root of the Oak, and now, craning his neck, he could see the solemn faces of the giant and his bride; but in the effort to keep his eyes on them, and thus compel attention, his neck was so taut and tense that his voice grew hoarse and thin like a gander's voice, scraping and scratching at his throat. It disappeared altogether, as if it were a stream in summer drought, before he had said the half of what he meant to say; and when Furbister and Bala knelt before him, to exchange their vows and receive his blessing, he uttered it with such malignity that Furbister in return snarled like a dog at a spitting cat, and Bala turned a little pale.

Liss refused to go to the wedding-feast, so Albyn left her and went straight to the palace. The bridal procession had to take a longer road, for Furbister and his wife must set foot in every field between the Oak Trees and the town, to promise it fertility; but Albyn, in whose mind were warring emotions, had no intention of sharing that roundabout and tedious progress. Though he was still perturbed about his quarrel with Liss, he had been delighted by the marriage ceremony, and he felt cheated because there was no one with whom he could share his delight. For who but Liss — and she was unfriendly and would not listen — could understand his pleasure at seeing a multitude of old, sweet, wrinkled apples listening to the nuptial hymn, and a wrathful gander commanding piety through a neck astrain and hissing beak? Only in a horn or two of mead could he resolve the conflict and forget his loneliness; and at the palace there would be a plenitude of mead.

He found a great stir and bustle there, and preparations to feast some three or four hundred people. On a level field before the palace, benches and trestle-tables had been set out, and at one side, behind a long screen of brushwood to break the wind, there were cooking-fires and pots slung over them, and roasting-dishes in turf-ovens, and some forty stout and cheerful women — the best cooks in all Galloway — prodding and tasting, supping gravy and heaping embers, sprinkling herbs and basting joints, seasoning and cosseting the beef and mutton, the hares and geese and piglings and fish, that would furnish the feast; and sweating as they worked. Then Albyn, with a horn of mead inside him and another in his hand, perceived quite suddenly how vastly superior were cooking-pots to a wedding, and cooks to brides and grooms; and began to make a speech about his perception to a couple of brawny old mothers of five, six, or seven children apiece who stood near him roasting a kid on a spit and boiling mutton in a pot.

'How wretched, how vile, is flesh without fire!' he said. 'What a squalling and dishevelled lump is man at birth, and in his middle years how dull and flavourless the man who has no flame to warm him! The child must go out into the sun, and men, to be whole men, need the heat of faith or the coals of art. They need what you're so clever at — a little blowing and raking and poking — for what you produce is finished, brown, succulent, and desirable; and so should we all be! Yes, fire's the essential factor, and because cooks have made fire their servant, so cooks should be acclaimed the masters — no, the mistresses! I like a mistress better! — the mistresses of life. God bless you, dear women! I'm more interested in the outcome of that pot than in the fruit of any womb alive. For one's the product of art and fire, the other a mere consequence of appetence and a hedgerow.'

The women whom he addressed were of mature age and mothers, in the aggregate, of a dozen children or so. They were aware of the importance of their work, but they knew also that a talented and robust young man, with a horn or two of drink in him, was not to be despised as a source of amusement. So they listened willingly enough, they laughed and encouraged him; and presently others joined them; and those farther off, fearing they might be missing something of value, came waddling, panting, and hurrying up, till in a few minutes Albyn was surrounded by all forty cooks, and a good many of the servants and minions whom they had told to stay and watch their pots and ovens.

'What good company I'm in,' he cried. 'Company after my own heart! For you are cooks and I'm a poet, and the only difference between us is that you do more than I, and do it better. I try to kindle fire, but you blow it or smother it as you choose. — How I envy your husbands! How you must turn them to the flame and baste them with desire! If your husband is cold you rake the embers above and beneath him, and in no time at all he's sizzling and smoking for your pleasure! If your man is young and tender, you know how to bring him quickly to the boil; and if he's old and tough, you let him stew and simmer till he's kind and palatable. Flesh without fire is only fodder for the worms, but a man with heat in him will please his wife and may please God as well. You cooks are teachers to us all, and delight us while you teach. I have seen Bala married, and care nothing for the upshot; but I've watched that tawny, brawny, lovely woman there basting a kid on her spit, and I'm all hunger for the consequence. God bless good cooks, I say!'

In this manner — but getting more broad and free in his reference as he went on — he talked for some while, and a few men of Furbister's household were attracted to the gathering. They, guessing that Albyn's eloquence would be encouraged by drink, hurriedly sent for a small tub of mead, and passing full horns about, made the speaker and his audience even merrier than they had been. Now Albyn had only to say, 'Dear cooks and sister-poets!' — and all the women would brandish their spoons and ladles, their tongs and long-handled forks, and beat upon their fat sides, and laugh as though they had heard the finest joke in the world. Their joints were smoking, their stews boiling over, their ovens red-hot, but no one gave them a thought till suddenly a word was spoken. — '*Furbister!* Furbister's here, and Bala, and the wedding-guests!'

Had they been less enthralled by Albyn's eloquence they would have heard long since the flute-players and the bagpipers who heralded the giants' approach; but now, taken by surprise, there was a shrill and startled hubbub, and while the cooks and their assistants — screaming and squealing, sniggering and scuttering — hurried back to neglected ovens and pots unstirred, Albyn sauntered slowly towards the meadows on the far side of the palace. The summer flowers had faded, but for his pleasure the hills before him rose in deepening colour to their gentle heights, and sunshine freckled the bay beneath. It would be prudent, he thought, to enjoy their beauty until, at the palace, confusion had been somewhat calmed.

He discovered, when he returned, that Furbister's butler and his pantrymen had cleverly diverted attention from the cooks' unreadiness by serving an abundance of ale, so that when the giant and his guests sat down, neither he nor they were aggrieved by the lateness of their dinner, or unduly critical because some joints were black as charcoal and others half-raw. The world itself seemed only to copy the butler and his pantrymen, for in their hands ale circulated like the earth about the sun, and mead followed as if it were the moon for ever girdling the earth.

In some inconspicuous position Albyn sat and ate, and drank enough to keep him lively; and when, by the rising tone of conversation, and increasing laughter from the table-end where Furbister and Bala sat, he decided that the time was ripe for a speech of congratulation, he rose from his place and approached the other end of the great table that twenty carpenters had been a month in making for the feast.

It was two ells broad and fifteen long. Tall trees had been split and their planks dovetailed and smoothly shaved to build it; and Furbister and Bala sat at the top with all their principal guests arrayed on either side. So that Furbister and his bride should be at an equal height with their friends, a pit had been dug in which the giants' huge chairs were set, and so lowered to the general level. Albyn, in high-flying mood, leapt upon the table at the far end, and horn in hand, announced, 'This is no day for common sentiments! Let's drink a toast to immoderation and superfluity!

'How dull would life be,' he declared, 'if all were equal! Could we abide our earth if every hill was measured to the same height, and the sea was like a level trough? How terrible would be a forest where all the trees were patterns of each other — and how tame the meadows if there was but one common flower! But that is not the way of nature. In nature there is infinite diversity, all obedient to certain rules, and because Furbister's a symbol of diversity — and Bala's another — let us be glad of them and rejoice. They're not immortal — that is too much to hope! Oh, far too much! — but within the little, little span of life they may remind us that we're all different, one from another, as tree from tree and ladies' fingers from wild thyme — and nature meant us so! I, when I look at them, feel more myself; and that's the greatest good they do. You also must feel something stirring that is yours alone, and should be grateful. So stir your stumps and rise and drink to Furbister and his bride — to glorious excess and our fortuitous lack of it!'

Now the wedding-guests to whom Albyn spoke had drunk so much they were willing to drink again to anything at all; and Furbister and Bala, being assured that no one would say anything that was not complimentary, were visibly moved by what they took to be his kindness. But Furbister and Bala, at the other end of the great table, were curiously situated. In the pit that had been dug for their great chairs the earth was soft, and beneath their prodigious weight their chairs had sunk till now their chins were on a level with the table-top. Furbister had grown a little fidgety as he subsided, but Bala, unaccustomed to such a quantity of mead as she had drunk, found it comforting to rest her cheek upon the board. Bala, when Albyn had finished speaking, murmured applause and let her head subside; but Furbister, tilting back his chair, stood up to reply.

To get upon his feet he had to press upon the table. He had to press hard and force himself up — and beneath his enormous weight the table-end sank into the pit in which his chair, and Bala's, had been set. Albyn, at the far end, leapt clear as it rose, and then the long board inclined towards the giant at an increasing angle, and down its slope — before he could say a word — slid the remnants and the debris of the feast. Beef-bones and ribs of mutton, the little splintered bones of hares, the glutinous vertebrae of cod and haddock, oyster-shells and the sharp hoofs of a pig's trotters — down they all came, and hastening their descent was the flood of ale and mead from horns upset and mugs turned over. One half of this rushing spate cascaded against the skirt of Furbister's wedding-robe, but the other half tumbled, as if over a waterfall, into the open gulf of Bala's gown, and down the deep valley of her prodigious bosom fell the shins of cows, the skulls of sheep, crusts of oatbread, drumsticks, and fish-bones, pigs' feet and oyster-shells — all carried on a mingled flood of ale and mead that drenched her to the knees and roused her, by its chill, to loud complaint.

Furbister, still leaning on the table and mustering his thoughts for speech, began to make some dignified statement of little meaning, but Bala, soaked to the skin, interrupted him and cried, 'I'm cold! I'm wet!'

'My dear,' said Furbister. 'I'm making a speech.'

'Get me a towel!' shouted Bala.

'You're over-wrought,' said Furbister, and bending towards her, with the kindest intention, raised and enfolded her in his great arms, and clasped her to his breast.

'Let go, let go!' she howled, writhing in his cruel embrace, for its pressure was driving a great rubbish-

heap of mutton-bones, shin-bones, fish-bones, pigs'
trotters, and oyster-shells into the huge softness of her
breast. — 'Let go, you fool!' — And as Furbister relaxed his grip, she swung a ringing slap to the side of
his head.

Furbister was astounded by the blow. Never before
had anyone so assailed his dignity; never before had
he known the pain of being slapped. For a little while
he stood breathing deeply, unable to speak, his face
mottled by fury and the blow; which had, indeed, been
heavy enough to fell an ox. Then he turned to the
wedding-guests and hoarsely exclaimed, 'Go! Go away!
And quickly!'

No one paused to be told a second time, and no one
dared look back. But before they had gone very far
they heard Bala's voice again, howling more loudly
than before.

CHAPTER ELEVEN

THE misunderstanding and the little display of
ill-humour that prematurely brought an end to
Furbister's wedding-feast were quickly forgotten, and the giant and his bride became the happiest
of married couples. Furbister had been lonely, and so
had Bala; he had wanted a companion capable of
robust affection, and she, like an unknown continent
awaiting its explorers, had dreamt of the hero who
should take advantage of her riches. Now both had
got what they wanted, and only the more sensitive of
their neighbours grumbled about the exuberance with
which they proclaimed their happiness. The more
critical observed with interest that Bala's influence
grew from month to month, that Furbister yielded
more and more to her judgment and her wishes; while
the philosophical perceived with gratitude that love
had turned his mind away from war.

The burden of feeding two giants was heavy, and
everywhere in Galloway Furbister's tax-gatherers were
for ever filching grain and cattle, ale and poultry, that
people could ill afford and might have kept for their
own use had their little kingdoms not been overwhelmed and united under so inordinate a government.
But all who had any tincture of wisdom were agreed
that Bala was a lesser burden than the wars which
Furbister had previously engaged in.

There was a melancholy but prudent man in the Isle
of Whithorn who summed the matter up, and whose
words were widely repeated. 'No one since our grand-

fathers' day,' he said, 'has been so innocent as to think he can live happily. The best we can hope for is a tolerable unhappiness; and to pay taxes to furnish Bala's table is better than shedding our blood to feed Furbister's desire of glory. It's a pity, of course, that our children can't eat as much as they would like to, or as much as they could get if there were no giants in the world and everybody minded his own business. But no one's starving, and we ought to be thankful for what we have.'

After the continual warfare of the years in which Furbister had been creating the kingdom, an interlude of peace was welcome indeed, even though it was expensive; and many of the younger people who could not remember an easier past, nor realize that their own clan had once been able to govern its own affairs, believed they were as well-off as anyone had a right to expect. They did not even resent taxation. 'Our dogs have worms and bluebottles feed upon our ewes,' they said, when Furbister's men drove off their cattle and demanded half their new-ground meal. 'The world is full of pests,' they told each other; and shrugged their shoulders.

Among the few who were positively unhappy in the first two years of Furbister's marriage were the Oldest Druid and Ferli. The Oldest Druid grew sour and spiteful as he watched the giants' contentment, and Ferli became as lonely as Bala had been in Northumbria. Bala, who had been her constant companion for nine or ten years, no longer needed her. Ferli had been proud of Bala — proud of her singularity, proud of Bala's dependence on her — and now Bala was no longer dependent and no longer singular. Bala was not even grateful, she had simply forgotten Ferli; and after a year of misery Ferli came to Liss and begged to be allowed to live with her. People in distress used always to go to Liss for help, and as she already had a dozen or more dependants in her house — twice it had had to be enlarged for them — Ferli's arrival made little difference. She was less attractive than when she rode from Rothbury, and Albyn, though kind enough, did not pay much attention to her.

Liss had borne her first child, a fat and lively girl, less than a year after marriage, and Albyn was delighted to be a father. Liss, now softly plump, was lovelier than ever before, and within a month or two the child had proclaimed its robustitude and gaiety. 'Match me such a poem!' he often challenged — having long forgotten his declared preference for the art of cooking — and when ballad-singers, flute-players, or bagpipers came to the house he would listen politely to their songs and tunes, and then, giving them ale to soften their defeat, fetch the baby from her cradle and show her off, as if to say: 'What are your verses and your melodies in comparison with this?'

He grew a little stouter, he was very idle, and he never apologized for his idleness or tried to conceal it. He would, indeed, defend it with a vigour that he rarely showed in any other cause; and once, when Liss had sharply told him that he ought to find some work to do, he retorted: 'Don't you see what a mistake that would be? Don't you realize that the greatest fault in life is to want too much? — It may even be a sin, but you'll have to ask the Druids about that. I've never pretended to know what goes on in God's mind. I'm quite satisfied to enjoy the pleasanter products of His ingenious hand: that's you, my dear, and the winter light on the sea, and the mutton-stew I've just eaten, and the child as pink as a mushroom, and those five swans that have just arrived to reinforce my argument.' — For at that moment five swans, making a hollow song in the hollow air, flew over them with heavy wings and necks like rods against the sky.

'I've got as much as I want,' said Albyn, 'and to work for more would be the height of folly. The object of working is either fame or riches — and how ungrateful it would be to want more riches than you, the swans, a mutton-stew, and a baby in the cradle! As for fame, that's a thing I've no interest in. Fame's only useful as a bandage to conceal some horrid wound. Let men who are unhappy go out and look for fame. So long as you're under my roof, I want none of it but what you give me. — Let's talk no more about such nonsense, but come indoors and I'll tell you what contentment is.'

Liss had a sense of duty, she had been taught responsibility, she was diligent, a stern critic of herself; but to Albyn she was very indulgent, though she did not go so far as to believe all he said. She knew every family within twenty miles of Wigtown, and was devoted to their welfare: day after day the sickly, the unfortunate, the bewildered, and the worthless were at her door for comfort or advice, and got both with equal generosity, though they made little use of the latter. — 'You're wasting your time,' Albyn would sometimes tell her. 'If you were kind only to the talented, such as ballad-singers and good flute-players, and to the handsomest and strongest people in the country, you'd encourage everyone to be talented, handsome, or strong. And that would make life very agreeable. — But as it is, you encourage weaklings and wastrels, the feckless and the shirtless, and purely out of charity you multiply the out-of-luck. There wouldn't be half as many cripples in the country — half as many paupers, children with ringworm, houses with leaky roofs, and beds without blankets — if you let it be known that in future you were only going to reward those who kept well and learnt how to look after themselves.'

'Then what would happen to a poor woman like Mart?' demanded Liss, one day when he had been talking in this manner and a wretched creature called Mart was waiting for some soup. 'Her children are half-starving.'

'So is her husband,' said Albyn. 'I know him quite well, and he lives a wretched life. Mart's the stupidest woman in the world, and quite useless to anyone!'

'Then someone has to help her. Surely that's obvious?'

'Why?'

'Well, she couldn't live, if no one helped her.'

'Then her husband might find a better wife, and his children would have a stepmother who could cook.'

'She might be cruel to them. Stepmothers often are.'

'That doesn't affect my argument — '

'No, dear. I wasn't thinking of the argument. I was thinking of the children.'

Albyn, impatient, was about to reply, when he realized that it would do no good; and went off in a temper. The King, who had been sitting with them in the hall, but taking no part in the conversation, said complacently, 'You had the better of him there.'

'I hadn't!' exclaimed Liss indignantly. 'Albyn was quite right, and I agreed with almost everything he said. His idea wouldn't work, of course — '

'That's what I meant,' said the King.

'But it was an interesting idea.'

'You're infatuated with the fellow.'

'I believe I am,' said Liss. 'And he's by no means indifferent to me.'

Twelve months after the birth of her first child, Liss was brought to bed of another daughter. — Albyn professed his lively pleasure, and the child indeed was a charming miniature of her mother's beauty. But his pleasure was echoed by too many people, for Liss now gave shelter to nineteen poor or distressed friends and relations — the house had again been enlarged — all of whom were loud and profuse in their appreciation of her achievement. Albyn, congratulating his wife and praising her second daughter, felt that he was only saying what had been said often enough already; and grew a little restless. Winter had gone, the days were long and light again. The house, so full of people, was oppressive, and he remembered with a sigh how free his life had been before he had a house. He thought of hill-roads, riverside roads, and roads that kept company with the sea; and decided that he could bear no longer the confinement of four walls and the smell of a peat-fire.

He told Liss that he was going on a journey; he wanted to see the western parts of Galloway. Liss, with the child at her breast, said she was sure it would do him good. He was looking pale, she said, and putting on too much weight. He needed exercise. 'How long will you be away?' she asked.

'A month, or perhaps two,' he answered, and felt a little jealous of his daughter. Had it not been for her, Liss would surely have been less agreeable to his going. — He set off, however, with a pleasure that grew from mile to mile, going south along the coast; and when he had gone no more than a couple of leagues he saw Ferli sitting at the roadside.

'Can I come with you?' she said.

It was the last week of April, and the sky was a veiled azure. Through the mat of winter grass, straw-pale and thin, green tufts were springing, and the cold sea crisped and curled upon the warmer sand. Redshanks were whistling their alarm, and a lamb with its tail in ecstasy was butting its mother's flank. The south wind blew, and a pair of lapwings tumbled and somersaulted in the kindly air.

Ferli was thinner than she had been when they rode from Northumbria, but much livelier than in the season of her unhappiness when Bala had forgotten her. There was more character in her face, a new tautness in her figure; the mole beside her chin was not really much of a blemish.

'When I am travelling,' said Albyn, 'I take whatever lodging is the handiest, and if none is handy I do without. I often walk far, and sometimes I lie hard.'

'No one needs me in Wigtown,' said Ferli. 'No one wants me, so far as I know. I'd like to see some other places. And you needn't worry about me. I can walk as well as you, and I'm sure I can sleep wherever you do.'

'The nights are cold.'

'They're getting warmer. Summer's coming.'

'I'll be in Wigtown again before the end of June.'

'We'll have the whole of May. I don't care what happens after that.'

'I'm the father of a family,' said Albyn stiffly —

'I thought you were a poet?'

'Even a poet must know his place in the world.'

'I'm only a woman. I'm thinking of my place in time.'

'Oh dear!' said Albyn. 'Have you become witty as well as good-looking? That makes it even more difficult. — I wish you hadn't come! We're bound to get into trouble. All our troubles are due to not walking alone. — I wish the wind would go into the north, and that lapwing would stop dancing!'

'I shan't come back if you don't want me to,' said Ferli.

'Don't pretend to be unselfish. You're thinking only of your own pleasure.'

'I'm willing to share my pleasure, and keep my trouble to myself.'

'If you can walk as well as you talk,' said Albyn, 'we're going to travel fast.'

'You'll let me come, then?'

'I wish I were sixty-five, and past temptation. But to be sixty-five with a life of perfect prudence behind one would make a dull evening to the day. — Yes, come along.'

Seven weeks later, in Stranraer, he woke one morning and found that she had gone. He lay for a little while and tried to persuade himself that this was good fortune. They were now on the homeward road, but he had said nothing of how their journey was to end. That was too difficult a problem; it could be put off until the last hour, when necessity might somehow

solve it. But Ferli, guessing that he did not want her
to return, had kept her word and left him. — An honest
girl, thought Albyn, and told himself again that his
luck was in.

He was in no hurry to start, however, and when the
sun showed him it was noon he was still waiting for
her to change her mind and come back. Then in a
great hurry, with a sudden fear indeed, he set out to
look for her; and a man working in the fields told him
where she was hiding. She had not gone very far.

'You'll get into worse trouble if you leave me,' he
said.

'What happens to me is no concern of yours.'

'That was true a couple of months ago, but it isn't
now.'

'I'm frightened of Liss,' said Ferli.

'So am I,' said Albyn.

'She'll forgive you, but not me.'

'It can be almost as painful,' said Albyn, 'to be forgiven as to be unforgiven. — Let us not think about it
till we have to.'

They walked steadily now — no longer loitering, as
they had done for weeks past — and in the late afternoon of the following day, about three miles from
Wigtown, they came to the house of a bagpiper with
whom Albyn was friendly; and there he left Ferli. He
went on alone, and felt a little more confident when it
occurred to him that there was no need for an immediate confession. It would, indeed, be the height of
discourtesy to greet his wife with the news that he
had been unfaithful to her. Far better to wait a few
days — or better, a few weeks — and then, when they
were at ease together and his journey was something

that had happened in the past, he might find occasion to tell her of his lapse in such a way as to make it seem a very small and unimportant matter. — Yes, that was his plan: he would put off confession for a month at least.

This prudent decision gave him so much comfort that he now looked forward with the utmost eagerness to meeting Liss; and he was unreasonably disappointed when he found the house deserted by all except a nurse, who was playing with his elder daughter, and a few of the more decrepit of Liss's aged relatives. Everyone else was at the palace, he was told, and had been there since noon. — No, the King was not ill, but there had been bad news of some kind.

He hurried to the palace, and met Liss coming from it. The Oldest Druid was with her, and a young nurse carrying the child. A little way behind them, moaning and crying, were some of the old men and women to whom Liss gave shelter. Albyn kissed her, and waited for the ill tidings.

'It is Bala's doing,' she said. 'Her appetite has grown with all she's eaten since she came here, and now she wants the sign of power as well as power itself. She's hungry for the crown, and Furbister has told my father he must abdicate.'

'What does he say?'

'He has refused. — But let us go home, for I am tired. We have been talking all day, and no one knows what to do.'

Later in the evening she told him the whole story: how Furbister, some six months ago, had demanded of the King to be named his heir, and how the King, after long argument, had sworn his councillors to secrecy and given Furbister the succession. 'It was only today that he told me,' said Liss, 'and now he's ashamed. He's ashamed because his weakness has done no good. He thought that by giving in to Furbister, he would assure peace in the kingdom for his own life-time at least. But he didn't know enough about Bala. He didn't know her greed, and her impatience. She waited all winter for him to die, and then she could wait no longer, so Furbister came back and asked my father to give up his crown. He was quite frank about his reason, and said it was to please Bala.'

'What is going to happen?'

'My father's very stubborn sometimes. He may give in, he usually does; but if he takes it into his head to be obstinate, there'll be trouble for us all — unless Furbister decides that trouble wouldn't be to his advantage. Will you go and talk to him?'

'Has the Druid seen him?'

'Furbister refused to listen. He's in a bad mood because of something that happened on the northern frontier a week ago.'

'A fight?'

'The fight was over before our people got there. He sent a company to punish the Ledi, who'd been stealing cattle again, and when the company arrived they found that soldiers from Carrick had got there first.'

'Poor Furbister,' said Albyn. 'He used to be so frightened of Od McGammon — but now, perhaps, he thinks Bala can protect him. I'll go and see him tomorrow. I've a present for him, an Irish knife that I got from a sailor in Stranraer. It'll do to cut his nails.'

There was a little pause, and then Liss inquired, 'Did you bring Ferli back?'

'What, what — ' he stammered.

'Surely you took her with you? She disappeared as soon as you had gone, and I thought you had probably arranged to go together. She had been even more restless than you for a long time.'

CHAPTER TWELVE

'YOU know what women are,' said Furbister moodily. 'They blow from all quarters, and when you're least expecting it they'll veer to the north-east. There's a cold persistence in them that you don't realize till you've lived with one for a couple of years. She'll make some proposal, let's say, that doesn't appeal to you, and you tell her so. — Very well; she changes direction, and the wind's in the south again. But not for long. Out of a clear sky it swings round, you suddenly feel cold, and she's blowing away at the old topic. — I don't want to be King of Galloway. I see no advantage in it. But Bala has set her heart on being Queen, and I can't enjoy talking to her as I used to. It doesn't matter what the subject is: I always find myself waiting for the little pause that'll give her a chance to veer or back, as the case may be, and then, sure enough, she's in the north-east again.'

'The Druids are against it,' said Albyn. 'The Oldest Druid was very bitter with the King yesterday, when he discovered that you'd been promised the succession. And the people won't like it, when they hear.'

'I pay no attention to the Druids; and I've never been able to see much importance in the people's likes and dislikes. They may go about with long faces, but they can't do anything.'

'It might be awkward,' said Albyn, 'if they made up their minds to do nothing.'

'What do you mean by that?'

'It depends on what Od McGammon means. He seems to be coming very close, and he may come closer. In that event, it would be disconcerting if the people of Galloway refused to resist him because the King of Galloway had already been deposed.'

There was a kind of loosening, a little sagging, in the contours of Furbister's great face, and hoarsely he inquired: 'What have you heard of Od McGammon? Did you meet anyone from Carrick when you were in the west?'

'Only a half-wit, who had run away. He said his wits had been good enough till a year or two ago, but they and his back had both been hurt because he refused to obey orders. — No, I know nothing about the King of Carrick except what I was told yesterday: that you had sent a company against the Ledi — '

'I should have done it a year ago, two years ago. I intended to; but then I had other matters to think of, and I put it off. They're nothing but cattle-thieves, the Ledi, but I only meant to punish them. I gave no orders to occupy their land; it's only hill-ground, useless for anything except to hide a parcel of thieves.'

'But Od McGammon has thought it worth his while to take it.'

'His troops were there when we arrived,' admitted Furbister. 'They told my company commander — a good fellow called Bure. Do you know him? — they told him they had destroyed the Ledi, because they were a danger to peace. They showed Bure some of the bodies, and he was very impressed. They'd done their work quite tidily, and their men were well disciplined. And Bure certainly got the idea that they meant to keep the ground they had won.'

'If that's the case, it either shows that Od McGammon is frightened of you, and means to watch what you're doing; or that he's planning to invade Galloway, and has chosen a convenient place to start from.'

'The probability is,' said Furbister with no conviction in his voice, 'that he's frightened of me.'

'You ought to make sure of that,' said Albyn, 'before you decide to upset the constitution of your own country. Don't be in too much of a hurry.'

'When you go to bed at night,' said Furbister, 'are you ever kept awake by a north-east wind in your ear?'

'In domestic life,' said Albyn, 'however happy it may be, there are certain strains and tensions that should, I think, be taken for granted. Chimneys smoke, servants won't get up in the morning, wives talk — '

'You can't ignore Bala, like a smoky chimney,' said Furbister.

'Why don't you separate for a month or two?' said Albyn. 'You might even persuade her to go to Carrick. As your ambassador to Od McGammon she would be very impressive, and if you sent a few of your cleverer people with her, they might learn something about his intentions; or, at the least, about his preparations.'

'She wouldn't go,' said Furbister. 'She's very timid, in many ways. She loses all her confidence when I'm not with her. — But the idea's good. I believe that's the thing to do! An embassy to Carrick to persuade Od McGammon that I'm anxious only to be on good terms with him; and, at the same time, to get the information about his military strength that I really need! Now who is there who could make a sufficiently good impression, and keep his eyes open too? — Would you go?'

'It's very kind of you,' said Albyn, 'but would Od McGammon take me seriously? Kings, and other people in authority, have a curious regard for age: they think that gravity consorts only with grey hairs, a bald head, a toothless jaw, or deaf ears — whereas gravity, of course, a passionate gravity, is the poisoned flower of youth, and old men are either delightfully cynical or abominably frivolous. But kings and their councillors are unaware of that, so you must look for someone twice or thrice my age. — And there's this to be added: that even if I were the proper sort of ambassador, my wife wouldn't let me go. Not alone. — I'm in a difficult position, Furbister, I've just been forgiven for a major fault, and a man who's forgiven is watched more closely than he who's unforgiven. If I were to propose another journey, my dear Liss — whom I adore — would say at once, "Then I am coming with you." And come she would, with nurses and children hard behind.'

'Take her,' said Furbister. 'Let her be my ambassador, with you in attendance on her. Od McGammon is King of Carrick by the right of birth, and Liss is a king's daughter. Her royalty will please him, and you'll have time to count his soldiers.'

'I have a better thought,' said Albyn. 'King speaks to King more closely than a king's daughter — therefore send Glam himself.'

'Would he go?'

'Tell him that Galloway's in danger, and you have changed your mind about his abdication. Tell him that peace depends on him; and he'll be flattered enough to leave his sea-shells for a month. Then you may tell Bala that war's a possibility, and she'll be frightened enough to let Glam keep his crown to bear the brunt of it.'

'Yes, that might quieten her for a little while, and if I can establish good relations with Carrick — but I must know what they're doing there! I want goodwill, but knowledge I must have. So if I persuade Glam to be my envoy, and promise peace, will you be my intelligence and see what chance we'd have in war?'

'That would suit me very well,' said Albyn, 'and I believe it would suit Liss, for we must go together, as I told you. New scenery would distract her, and if the inhabitants of Carrick are interesting, they may occupy her attention to my benefit. — I should much prefer my recent fault to be forgotten than forgiven. — So I shall work on her, while you work on Glam, and if we go as a family party, a Royal family, with nurses, children, and so forth in our train, Carrick will never suspect you of including a few spies among the grooms and soldiers who attend us. Spies travel singly, stealthily and swiftly, but we shall be a large and distinguished party, moving slowly and with a certain pomp and display; we shall inspire confidence from the start, and before the end, perhaps, win Carrick's love, and his people's reverence. — I congratulate you, Furbister, on your plan. It's masterly. Do you mind if I move my stool into the shade?'

'A good discussion clears the air,' said Furbister complacently. 'I think we've solved our difficulties — '

'You must remember to frighten Bala.'

'I'll speak seriously to her, I'll let her know the situation. — Are you more comfortable there?'

'It's cooler, out of the sun.'

'We must have been talking for an hour or more.

It's noon! It's noon, and there's no one here. — Boy!' he roared. 'Boy!'

A little fellow came out of the palace, and Furbister said: 'Tell my butler to bring the mead, the cask I told him to put in the stream to cool. And horns, the larger horns: bull's horns!'

CHAPTER THIRTEEN

THE King grumbled for a week, but a fierce and retributive assurance of his own importance had swelled his heart from the day when Furbister, uncommonly affable, came with his request; and the King, after some little argument, had understood its purport. For his dignity's sake he had protested for seven days that the mission was beneath his dignity, but he had in fact resolved to undertake it in the very first moment after comprehending it; and the delay was useful to Albyn, who found more difficulty than he had anticipated in persuading Liss to accompany them. Liss would not be convinced that far travel was good for children in their infancy, though Albyn told her, again and again, that he himself had spent the first two or three years of his life in a shawl on his mother's back, as she trod the country roads in rain or sunshine, with the frost biting her heels or the west wind buffeting her cheeks.

'But what future have your children if they never budge from the room where they were born?' he demanded. 'The elder, if Furbister falls over a cliff and leaves the succession open, may in time become a queen. Nothing nobler than that, you say — but what of the others? Mere pendants of royalty, without a throne to sit on or common ground to stand on! Icicles hanging from a lordly roof, glittering in the sun, a dazzle in the common eye — but ah, so brittle! Let them be brought up, however, not in a palace, but in a shawl on the warm back of a young and healthy nurse, kicking against her shoulder-blades, sweating in the afternoon or shivering in the morning mist, and they may, like me, grow into poets. A family of poets! And the eldest, the heiress of Galloway, will be queen and a poet too! She's my daughter, and if you let the wind play on her forehead, and her toes learn to scramble in the runnel of that good girl's back — she may be a poet, I say, and dispense poetry from the throne. What do you say to that?'

'It sounds most improbable.'

'You may be right,' admitted Albyn with a sigh. 'Genius is rare, very rare. It needs more than good parents and fresh air to bring it on. Nevertheless — '

'Could we take a cow?' asked Liss.

It was an unusual addition to an embassy, said Albyn, but if there was good reason for it —

There was a red cow with a white saddle and white socks on whose milk, she explained, their elder child was thriving wonderfully; if it could come too, she might undertake the journey.

In that case, he assured her, the cow should accompany them; though they would have to ride slowly so as not to tire her.

But Liss was still undecided, and with a sudden change of subject, asked him how often he had been to see Ferli. — Only twice, he answered, to make sure that she was comfortable with the bagpiper and his wife; and added with some complacency that she seemed to be contented and was much improved in her appearance.

On the following day Liss went to see for herself if Ferli's journey to the west had so enhanced her looks; and was bound to admit that it had. Ferli cried, pleaded for forgiveness, and behaved exactly as she should have done. Liss, who was always honest, thought her very attractive, and considered again the embassy to Od McGammon. Common sense's counsel was that Albyn might be safer in Carrick than in Galloway; prudence advised her to make sure of it by going with him. And perhaps he was right, she thought: perhaps travel and fresh air were good for children.

She walked home, and told Albyn she would go to Carrick with him. — Furbister had already made all arrangements for the journey, and there was no difficulty in adding a dairymaid and a cow to his ambassador's retinue. The dairymaid wept, for she had newly found a sweetheart from whom she must now be parted; but no one gave her any sympathy, and with as little delay as possible the embassy set forth. In front rode six soldiers of the escort, then came the King with two of his councillors, and two Druids to represent the spiritual power of the Kingdom. Liss followed, riding between Albyn and the captain of the escort, and immediately behind them trudged two strong young nurses, each with a child on her back. A dozen pack-ponies, laden with food and blankets, were led by pioneers who would make camp and build turf-shelters for the travellers; and behind them rode a couple of cooks. Then came the dairymaid, leading her red and white cow, and last of all the remaining six soldiers of the escort, who amused themselves by making improper remarks to the dairymaid.

Their path climbed slowly into the hills, and their progress was slow. The children required much attention, the cow's feet were tender, and the King, who went to bed early, rose late. It was not until the morning of the fourth day of their journey that they came into the ravaged country of the Ledi, and saw how Od McGammon dealt with cattle-thieves. There was a little copse of twisted pines to the right of the path, and spread-eagled among their reddish branches were six dead bodies with drooping heads. — Liss and the young nurses cried out in horror, and looked the other way; but the captain of the escort was deeply puzzled, for he had expected to see many more bodies nailed to the trees. Od McGammon's men, he thought, had killed all their prisoners.

When they were well past the pine trees, and to windward of them, they halted for their midday meal but had no time to eat it. Suddenly, from the heather on either side, there rose a numerous company of well-armed men who came charging down upon them, shouting fiercely. The soldiers and the pioneers, taken by surprise, snatched up their weapons and fought half-heartedly; but in their confusion had no chance against a properly disposed and more numerous enemy. Liss, crouching in the heather, clutched her babies to her breast, the nurses screamed, and Albyn ran towards a short, broad-shouldered man who seemed to be in command of their assailants.

'We are an embassy from Furbister of Galloway to the King of Carrick,' he cried. 'This is no way to treat ambassadors!'

The broad-shouldered man looked coldly at him, but made no reply; and before Albyn could say another word an unseen enemy, behind him, hit him cruelly on the head with a heavy club.

Later, the man who had struck him was severely punished for hitting too hard. His orders had been to hit lightly so as only to stun; and then the captives, quickly recovering, could march without further trouble to their captors. But Albyn might have been killed, had his skull been less obdurate, and when he recovered his senses he found himself tied to one of the pack-ponies, his head hanging down on one side, his heels on the other. He was in great pain, and began to groan and vomit. He heard a voice say, 'He's all right, he's still alive'; but no one came to help or comfort him. Some time later he was untied and lifted from the pony, and carried, not unkindly, to a heap of straw; where he fell asleep.

When he woke he saw that he lay in a large field surrounded by a high turf wall. A few other men, wounded or ill, lay in a litter of straw under the walls, and a couple of idle soldiers strolled to and fro. But otherwise the field was empty until evening, when a great crowd of men marched in, a long untidy column that presently broke up and gathered again in little groups and clusters. They stood talking until food was brought. Then cooking-fires were lighted, a haze of smoke lay above the field in the summer darkness, and an old shuffling man gave Albyn a bowl of soup and an oat bannock. As soon as they had had their supper, the newcomers sought their beds under the walls, where straw was thickly spread, and lay down yawning and grumbling. But long after those on either side of him were snoring, Albyn, sleepless and utterly bewildered by all that had happened, was weeping for what Liss might be suffering.

It was nearly noon when he woke. He felt much better, and very hungry. He sat up and saw the old shuffling man who had brought him soup the night before. The old man waved to him, then turned away; but soon came back with a little bowl of milk.

'You are going to recover,' he said in a gentle voice. 'You have a good thick skull, and that is one of the greatest gifts a man can enjoy. A quick and capacious brain is a splendid endowment, but so often it's covered only by thin and tender bone — and what use is it then, if it meets with some little accident, the tap of a stick, or so forth? I've got a great admiration for a good brain, but just as much for a thick skull. You're a very lucky young man!'

Albyn drank his milk and asked, 'What place is this?'

'One of the Institutes for Friends from Over the Border,' said the old man. 'Most of your companions are here, but among so many strangers I suppose they feel confused and so on, and haven't been able to find you.'

'What are they doing? Why were we brought here?'

'To work,' said the old man. 'So long as skin sweats, a man must work for what he gets.'

'But we came as an embassy to Carrick. An embassy from Galloway to the King of Carrick.'

'Ah, but there's no King of Carrick now. It's two years since Od McGammon declared that all the lands of Carrick, Arran, Bute and the Two Cumbraes, Ayr and Renfrew, over which he rules, belonged wholly and solely to the people who dwelt therein, and that he was merely their guardian. Then, for the sake of brevity and convenience and so forth, he told us that our territories would be known henceforth as Greater Carrick, and his humble title, as the servant of the people, would be the Caretaker of Carrick.'

'And who is your ruler now?' asked Albyn.

'Od McGammon, of course. The poor, ignorant people who own the land are quite incapable of looking after it and so on — even incapable, he explained, of looking after themselves — and therefore his duties as Caretaker are much more onerous than those of a king. For kings are selfish creatures, but Caretakers must have a sense of duty and recognize historical necessity and natural law, and so on and so forth. They are, in short, extremely active.'

'What has happened to my King? Glam of Galloway?'

'He was very troublesome, and refused to work. He said it was beneath his dignity, that he never had worked, and had no intention of starting now. So he was removed to another of our institutes: The Institute for the Reinstatement of Necessary Ideas.'

'He had a daughter,' said Albyn. 'Her name was Liss. She had two children.'

'There were four women in your party,' said the old man. 'They suffered no hurt, you can be assured of that; nor did the children. Women and children are well treated in Carrick.'

His voice was very soft and gentle, and he spoke with a smile, as though he were perpetually amused by what he said or by himself for saying it. His face was small and wrinkled, he had a shock of white hair and very bright blue eyes. Albyn, who himself looked like a natural, was well disposed to people whose minds had taken a path of their own; the old man, he thought, was something of a simpleton.

'Tell me about yourself,' he said.

'My name is Parr,' said the old man. 'I was a

Druid until Od McGammon abolished superstition and disestablished our order; and now I sweep up the field, and take soup to people who aren't well. Many of my colleagues, of course, refused to submit to the King — he was still a king at that time — and they, poor souls, were burnt to death. But I've always been rather timorous, even cowardly, I suppose, and because I was very much afraid of being burnt, and quite terrified by the prospect of death, and so on and so forth, I'm afraid I gave in to him. If God, I thought, has created giants and let them live, He ought to let His cowards live too. — But no! That's not quite true. I only thought of that later. All I thought of at the time was that I couldn't stand the pain of being burnt alive. So I became a sweeper instead. — But you don't want to hear about me, you want to be told about Od McGammon. And I've nothing to do till the men come back from the fields, so make yourself comfortable, and so on, and I'll tell you what I know about him; or, at any rate, what I've heard.'

'OD McGAMMON'S mother,' said Parr, 'was Princess of Arran in her own right. She was his father's third wife, who by the time he married her was already known as the Old King. He was a fortunate, gifted, merry, and burly man who, from the age of twenty-five or so, had very seldom been quite sober after sundown, and rarely gone without a woman he desired. His first two wives brought him great territories in Ayr and Renfrew, and most of their revenue he spent on his own pleasure. He had so many illegitimate children that the few who were born in wedlock felt quite inferior, and without exception were meek and dispirited — until Od was born. He, from his first appearance, was manifestly different, and his poor mother died of the difference. But not only was he greater in size than his half-brothers and sisters: his spirit was rebellious, and when he was twelve years old he publicly rebuked his father for drunkenness, lechery, and the maladministration of the royal lands.

'The Old King thought this the best of jokes, sold another farm, and gave a feast to celebrate Od's birthday. Od made a speech in which he said that all mankind was depraved, and he was going to reform it; and the King's friends, who were merry men like himself, laughed so loudly that the poor young giant blubbered for a week and sulked for a month. But two years later, when he came of age, Od claimed as his own the Principality of Arran, and went there as its ruler. — Now listen to what he did.

'Arran is a great island, but its people are few. They are shepherds and fishermen. The fishermen live in villages such as Loch Ranza, Brodick, Whiting Bay, Blackwater Foot, and so on and so forth; of which Loch Ranza is the biggest. So Od McGammon built a house there, and after he had lived in it for a year he discovered that nature was very disorderly, and men were as bad as nature. For in some places the summer grass grew lush and high, and was full of flowers, and the bees were drunk with sweetness like the old men about his father's court; and it made him angry to see such richness and enjoyment of life. But in other places there was sourness, and black heather, and bare rock; and because he himself was lonely he hated the desolate places almost as much as the little glens that smelt of honey.

'He discovered, too, that some of the fishermen were much better off than others; and the better-off were in general those who were clever and industrious and self-seeking. Nothing was done to prevent such men from working as long as they cared to, or from fishing far off the land in dangerously open water. And these greedy and reckless men lived in a fashion that quite put to shame their quieter neighbours, who only fished when the weather was fine, and even then were sensible enough to stay near the shore. The greedy men were fatter than the others, their families lived more comfortably, and often, after a good catch of fish, they would drink too much, and behave with impropriety, and so on and so forth. At such times, indeed, their behaviour was not unlike that of the Old King and his friends. And often from a full boat they would give some of their fish away, carelessly and even impatiently — a score of herring to this one, a big codling here, a basinful of whiting there. And though their poorer neighbours appeared to be grateful, Od McGammon felt sure they must be deeply humiliated by the fine gifts they received.

'Now what happened next is said to have been the consequence of a heavenly vision in which he was instructed how to change completely a way of life that was manifestly unjust, and therefore doomed to extinction; but many people think that cannot be true, because Od McGammon has said there is no such place as heaven. The simple facts are that he called a meeting of all the men in Loch Ranza, Brodick, Blackwater Foot, Whiting Bay and the other villages, and declared that in future the herring they caught and the corn they grew would no longer be the property of those who fished and reaped, but the common wealth of all who lived in Arran; and must be divided equally between them.

'Now this was easy enough to say, but hard to bring about; and many of the farmers and the fishermen had to give up farming and fishing to count and weigh what the others caught and harvested — and to count the people who were entitled to a share, and divide the herring and the halibut, the onions and the barley, equally between them; and deliver it at regular intervals so that none should want; and so on and so forth.

'Well, to begin with, there were very few — and they were the thinnest people — who could understand why all this was necessary, or see how it would benefit them; and a good deal of quarrelling occurred. Then there was more trouble when Od McGammon said that fishermen's wives must be common property just as much as the whiting and the haddock, the flounders and the cod they brought ashore; because, he explained, the materialistic and self-seeking men had married good, sturdy wives who were a great help to them, but the weaker sort had taken up with frail and idle creatures who did them no good at all. — For a fisherman's wife, you know, should gather bait for her husband, the limpets and the lugworms and so forth; and then she's expected to carry her husband through the shallow water to his boat, when he's putting to sea, so that he can go to sea with dry legs and feet. — Well, it was the women who objected most strongly to this new decree, and most of them refused point-blank to gather limpets for a man they did not love, and give a pick-a-back to comparative strangers. So Od McGammon had to find a number of thin young men to teach the women that equality required a lot of sacrifice; and some stronger men were needed too, to show them that a social duty could not be evaded. — But none of these plans would have worked if Od McGammon, in the nick of time, hadn't discovered something that no one had ever dreamt of before; something they might have gone to their graves without knowing, if it hadn't been for him.

'He called another great meeting, and told them the news. They were all in the utmost danger, he declared! At any moment, he said, Arran might be invaded by the arrogant and ambitious clans of Kintyre, who lived over in the west; or by the lawless and hungry people of Bute and the Two Cumbraes in the north. To live as they were doing, without a care in the world, was to invite disaster — especially from the Two Cumbraes, which were notoriously savage islands. Their only hope of safety lay in proper organization, and anyone who opposed his will to the well-being of the whole community would be recognized as a traitor and treated accordingly. They must accept their responsibilities, said Od McGammon; and immediately he set about the raising and training of an army to defend their shores.

'Well, everyone was desperately frightened to think that Arran might be invaded at any minute, and the women couldn't sleep at night for wondering what would happen if some furious man from the Two Cumbraes should come in through the door, and find them all alone, and so on and so forth; and Od McGammon had no difficulty in raising an army. But when he had taken two or three hundred men from their boats and their ploughs, and set them drilling in the fields — in addition, of course, to all those whose duty it was to count the herring and weigh the meal, to number the people, and go round with the fish, and teach the women the elementary rules of equality, and protect the teachers from those that got angry — when all these crying needs had been supplied, there was only one boat left to go to sea.

'Now Od McGammon had made the best of plans, and even on the days when not a fish was caught, it was share-and-share alike for all. So no one could grumble about inequality, though some did complain of hunger. They gathered nettles and dandelions and so on and so forth, but that was a windy diet; and a cod's head among four, they said, was only a mockery. A few of them went so far as to say that equality of sacrifice could never take the place of a good square meal — but just when it seemed that dissatisfaction was spreading, and might become serious, Od McGammon again showed the genius that was in him.

'He took the fishing-boats that no one used any longer, and turning his army into a fleet, sent it off on a defensive expedition against the Two Cumbraes. The inhabitants of those little islands, it turned out, were the mildest and most harmless of people, and the whole male population was brought back to Arran with their wrists tied together and great cries of acclamation. They were all skilful fishermen, and Od McGammon set them to work at once, with a few soldiers to guard them. They made good catches, and presently the people of Arran were eating nearly half as much as they had been used to in the past; and Od McGammon's policy was completely justified.

'A year or so later his father died; and paying no attention to the feeble claims that some of his older brothers put forward, he ascended the throne of Carrick. Without loss of time he organized the whole kingdom according to the system that had proved so successful in Arran, and whenever he found himself faced by a shortage of labour, he either made war on a neighbouring territory, and put his captives to work; or condemned some of his own subjects, for their own good, to a year or two of compulsory toil on essential tasks.

'And now, in consequence, Carrick's a large and powerful state, and Od McGammon has rewarded his people for their loyal service and hard work by renouncing the throne, transferring his titles to the kingdom to the whole community, and accepting on its behalf the office of Caretaker.'

'How have the people profited by that?' asked Albyn.

'Oh, not at all,' said Parr. 'Unless you count discretion a virtue? Everybody's very careful about what they say nowadays, in case someone should hear them, you see. — Everybody except me, that is. I'm just an old chatterbox.'

CHAPTER FIFTEEN

ON the following day Albyn was set to work, and for two days laboured with a dozen other prisoners carrying stones out of a field. None of the Galloway men was in his company, and when night came he was too tired to look for them. But on the third morning, when he was about to march off with the others, an official of the Institute for Friends from Over the Border came and led him to the large house in which the affairs of the Institute were conducted. He was to go to Ayr, he was told, and the old man called Parr gave him a clean shirt and a decent plaid. 'It's the Caretaker himself who has sent for you,' said Parr, 'and he's sure to ask you a lot of questions, and so on and so forth. Now be careful how you answer him, and remember this: that all men have equal rights in Carrick, but there's no equality in the wrongs they suffer.'

A sturdy-looking soldier was to be Albyn's escort, and after they had marched for a mile or two Albyn asked him, 'What language do you speak?'

'The same as you,' said the soldier.

'Then what shall we talk about?'

'Nothing,' said the soldier; and Albyn would have found the journey dull had it not been for the several villages through which they passed, where he saw much to interest him and occupy his thoughts. Od McGammon, it appeared, took care of his people with the utmost zeal, and many of them were employed only in furthering his benignity and making sure that none escaped it.

For the convenience of administration the giant had removed his court to Ayr, and it was late before they reached the town; where the soldier had some difficulty in finding his way. Many of the houses were being pulled down, and everywhere there was great confusion; but this, they learnt, was merely the result of Od McGammon's recent decision to rebuild his capital in a superior style and according to a better plan. After much inquiry they arrived at the house for which they were looking, which stood apart from its neighbours and was guarded by half a dozen soldiers. Albyn's escort reported their arrival to the Commander of the Guard, who told Albyn to go indoors.

He stood for a moment, a little blinded by the dusk of the room, and before he could quite recover his sight he heard a cry of happiness, and Liss came running to embrace him. They clung to each other, as if too weak with joy to stand alone, and spoke their love in broken sentences. They inquired with anguish of the other's suffering, and reassured themselves with tender lips and hands that pressed more closely. Then a querulous voice divided them: 'Did you hold your own against these ruffians? Or did you give in?'

Over Liss's shoulder Albyn saw the King sitting in a corner, and peeping through a doorway that led to an inner chamber were the two young nurses, with a child apiece. 'So we are all together!' he exclaimed.

'All together again,' Liss repeated fondly. 'And the cow's here too; she's in the yard.'

'Will you answer my question?' said the King.

'I had to work for two days,' said Albyn —

'The more fool you! They'd the impudence to try that game on me, but I told them who I was and made them feel silly. "I've come to see that giant of yours," I told them, "and the sooner I've seen him the better I'll be pleased. Because then I can go home again."'

The King, it appeared, had been most resolute, not only in refusing to do any work, but in his insistence that he and Liss were entitled to the same consideration in Carrick as they were accustomed to in Galloway. He and his two councillors and the Druids — the older men of the party — had been taken with the women to an Institute smaller than that which had received the others; and the authorities there had been much impressed, though unwillingly, by his evident authority. News of their arrival had been sent to Od McGammon, who had returned instructions that they were to be brought with all possible speed to Ayr; and they had seen him that afternoon.

'What is he like?' asked Albyn.

'Just the same as Furbister,' said the King. 'A big ungainly brute with no manners, a rank smell, and a brain like a duck's. He quacks at you, and says the same thing over and over again. They're all alike, these giants.'

'I don't agree,' said Liss. 'He's cleverer than Furbister, and much worse. He asked a hundred questions, and told us nothing.'

'What has happened to the others?' asked Albyn.

'They are being properly looked after, he said.'

'I had to carry stones all day.'

Od McGammon had offered no apology for his servants' rude treatment of the embassy, but promised that those who were to blame for it — if there were such — would be punished. Then he had inquired the reason for their coming into Carrick, and it had been difficult to persuade him that they had no other motive than to assure him of Furbister's friendship for his country. 'Why,' he had asked, 'should Furbister feel friendly towards me? No one else does.'

They had been well treated, however, and the house set apart for them was large and handsome. Mats of closely plaited grass covered the inner surfaces of the walls, there were clean rushes on the floor, and a stone fireplace in the largest room. In a smaller chamber Albyn and Liss slept comfortably on a great pile of sheepskins, saffron-dyed; but at midnight they were roused by loud shouting and hammering on the outer door. — Albyn had been granted an audience by the Caretaker.

'So far,' said Albyn, 'I haven't asked for one.'

'That is immaterial,' said the officer standing in the darkness.

Albyn was reluctant to leave the comfort of his bed for the nervous tedium of talking to a giant, but he felt it would be tactless to refuse the summons. So off he went, ill-humoured and a little anxious, and the officer who had come for him maintained an immaculate silence all the way to Od McGammon's palace.

In the summer darkness its enormous bulk was black and menacing, but when the ponderous doors were opened — split pine trees, bolted together, that three men could hardly move — the interior was half-full of a reddish uncertain light. They went in, and Albyn saw that on either side of the great hall stood men with torches in their hands, whose smoky flame wavered in the draught and gave off a fishy smell; for the torches had been steeped in the oil of cods' livers.

At the far end of the hall, on a platform three steps higher than the common level, the Caretaker sat in a massive chair with eight or ten of his advisers and chief officials about him, and a dozen torch-bearers enclosing them in a half-circle of florid light.

Albyn mounted the steps, and bowed. The giant sat huge and motionless, like a sea-cliff hollowed by the centuries, but the restless torches cast flickering shadows on his vast melancholy face, and the craggy knuckles of his enormous hands, that lay ponderous on the promontory of his knees, shone in and out of darkness like sheep moving slowly on a far hillside. At last he spoke, and his voice was harsh and high and shallow as the quacking of a duck.

'Give him a stool,' he said.

A stool was brought, and Albyn sat down. Again there was long silence, and then the Caretaker inquired, 'How big is Furbister?'

Albyn, somewhat ill-at-ease but out of humour also, had been watching the giant's white knuckles, that were like the backsides of sheep grazing distantly in sunshine and shadow; but now, looking up towards the flattish, pale expanse of Od McGammon's monstrous face, he saw that it was painted below the eyes with the dark blue pigment that the Druids used when they pretended to speak in the name of God. This was Furbister's habit, and though Albyn had grown accustomed to his presumption, he resented Od McGammon's. He answered hardily: 'Furbister, I should say, is taller than you by two hands.'

'Impossible!' cried the Caretaker in his quacking voice, and rose heavily to his feet. 'Think again,' he said, 'and tell me how big he is.'

'Two hands taller than you,' said Albyn. 'Perhaps two and a half.'

The Caretaker sat down, and after thinking for several minutes, inquired, 'If he is bigger than I am, why does he want to be friends with me?'

'In spite of his strength,' said Albyn, 'he has a mild nature and a kindly heart. His desire is to live at peace with all who do not wilfully offend him.' He described at some length Furbister's gentle character, and spoke so well that he found time, between two sentences, to reflect: I could almost believe my own words! And if that is so, I must be making a great impression on these others. — At this point, however, the Caretaker interrupted him.

'I saw your King today,' he said, 'who told me that he hoped there would be peace between Galloway and Carrick because there always had been peace, and he doesn't see what good can be served by war. — That, however, means nothing. It means only that he is an old man who doesn't want to be disturbed. — But when I asked him if there was much talk of war in Galloway, he said that Furbister had been talking about nothing else for days and days. For days and days — that's what he said.'

'Furbister has been a little worried lately. He sent a company against the Ledi, not long ago — '

'Is that how a peaceful man behaves? Is it? Is it? Does a man whose nature's mild and affectionate attack his neighbours?'

'They had been stealing cattle — '

'It's easy to make excuses,' said the Caretaker contemptuously. 'Tell me Furbister's excuse for plotting to take your King's throne. Tell me that.'

'Surely Glam said nothing of that?'

'Glam lied to me, as you have been lying; and denied it. Denied it outright. But his councillors are old fools who talk, when they're alone, like women in the market-place; and my servants have two good ears apiece. Two good ears on each of them.'

'There's no truth in the story. Furbister has no wish for the throne, and never had. But Bala wanted to be a queen, and for a little while he listened to her —'

'No one has told me about Bala. Who is she, eh? Who is she?'

'His wife.'

'How big is she?'

'A head shorter than Furbister.'

'Describe her.'

Here, thought Albyn, was a safer topic. So long as he said nothing of her greedy ambition, there would be no need to remember his duty and lie about her: the inordinate truth would satisfy even a giant. So speaking in his liveliest and most ample style he made a handsome picture of the vast expanses, the oceanic movement, the prodigious rotundities and awful de-clivities of her spectacular figure; and mentioned also her hearty appetite and boisterous disposition. Od McGammon listened with close attention.

'Describe her again,' he commanded when Albyn had finished.

Albyn, a little surprised, but pleased by the success of his eloquence, repeated his tale and improved it in several particulars. Od McGammon, leaning back in his chair with his hands clasped under his chin, fetched a sigh from his deep chest. 'I should like to hear that again,' he said.

So a third time Albyn told him about Bala, and now, being somewhat tired, he spoke more slowly and more quietly, and it seemed as if the giant limbs he described were relaxed in sleep, and Bala's great head, pillowed on a convenient hill, was docile under a clouded moon, her breast a Border landscape in its powdering light.

There was a long silence when he came to an end; and then the Caretaker murmured, 'He has a wife! I did not know he had a wife. A man may find a wife to mitigate his loneliness, but giants, I thought, who are forty times as lonely, must endure their solitude. I had not heard, till now, of such a one as Bala.'

The torches were guttering, and some had gone out. The smell of fish-oil had grown stronger, and threads of a pallid light shone through the crevices of the great door. None of Od McGammon's officials, none of the torch-bearers, had moved or spoken during the audience, but now, like the tetchy breeze that sometimes blows at the turn of the tide, there sounded a medley of small and hardly distinguishable noises: feet shuffling, joints creaking, tired breath snoring, a belly rumbling, a sleepy chorus of stifled yawns. — 'Open the doors,' exclaimed Od McGammon in the voice of an angry duck.

Groaning on their hinges, the great doors were thrust open, and the remnant torches flickered smokily as the cold air blew in. Albyn looked round and saw the pale sky of dawn as if he were in a cave and looking at the grey-glimmering sea.

'The audience is concluded!' said Od McGammon.

CHAPTER SIXTEEN

'I'VE taken half-a-liking to him,' said Albyn later in the morning, and stretched himself contentedly on his bed of saffron sheepskins. 'I told him about Bala, and he has fallen in love with my description of her.'

'You like anyone who will listen to you,' said Liss.

'I'm inclined to,' Albyn agreed. 'I've always been attracted to intelligence.'

'You like what interests you, or amuses you, or flatters you,' said Liss. 'You have no real love of people. You look at the ordinary people in their cottages or in the fields, and if a girl has good eyes and a quick smile — or a man has a bold red face, a ready turn of speech — you say you like them. But you like them, not for what they are, but because they please your imagination.'

'I am in love with you,' said Albyn. 'I have given my heart away to perfection, and so for the others I have nothing left but a mild indulgence.'

Liss paid no attention to him, and went on: 'You say you are fond of Furbister. He's gross and brutal and destructive, but it amuses you to look at his great knees and arms, that are like a mockery of human limbs. It pleases you to argue with him and get your own way, because it flatters you to match your brain with a brain that moves the body of a giant. — And now your pleasure's doubled, because you have Od McGammon to entertain you; though he's more evil than Furbister. And to say that you're fond of him means you have no principles, but only an appetite for pleasure.'

Liss rose indignantly from her bed, and with impatient movements belted on her dress. Albyn, scratching his head, sat up and asked, 'Why do you speak so bitterly about my pleasure?'

'You're not serious,' she said. 'And there are times when it's necessary to be serious.'

'I am serious in my own way. I'm serious enough when I wake in the morning and look at you; when I look at the white hair of a wave in winter, or a swarm of goldfinches in a thistle-field, or the mountain-hue of a horn of mead. I'm serious about good things,' said Albyn, 'but I've always felt that foolish and pretentious things were made for my amusement; and so I like them for that reason, and don't bother to make a solemn face at them. Nor do I bother much about common, dusty things, for I know all about them. I was well brought-up, you see. I lived in a house that had no walls, but plenty of furniture and a fine roof. It was furnished with all manner of common things and comical things — I learnt to walk by holding on to them — but my roof was the light of the whole sky. And by the time I was four or five I was beginning to suspect that some things were of more value in the world than others.'

'You're not serious enough,' said Liss.

'I shall be some day. I'll fill a grave, and look like it, as well as the next man. — Come back to bed.'

'I must go to the children.'

Albyn lay down again and spoke to the timbered roof above. 'A woman can be devoutly self-indulgent,' he said, 'and regard the gratification of her own desires as the proof of their high consequence.'

He fell asleep again, and after dinner walked with Liss, her father, the nurses and the children, on a sandy shore. Od McGammon had provided them with good servants, an abundance of food, and they were free to go where they pleased. They had to provide their own conversation, however, for the people they encountered were taciturn beyond belief. They were hard-working, and usually worked under supervision; but they were fairly well nourished, and appeared to be tolerably contented.

At midnight Albyn was roused again from his bed, and summoned by Od McGammon to another audience.

The scene was the same as before; torchlight in the great hall, and the giant in his chair immobile as a sculptured cliff. Their conversation was very nearly the same as before, and Albyn had again to describe the alluring amplitude of the young giantess whom Furbister had married. When he returned, at dawn, to his own house, he told Liss: 'In time, I think, one might grow tired of Od McGammon.'

That afternoon the giant commanded his company on the shore; and Albyn found him, alone, in a little wood that grew down to the sandy fringe of a small bay, with a view across the gleaming firth of Arran's blue gown and ragged crest.

'It was there,' said the giant, 'in that island you see, that I began to rule. Now I no longer rule, as kings understand it. I take care of my people — I take care of them in every way — and make them do whatever may be necessary for their own good.'

'They work harder than our folk in Galloway,' said Albyn.

'They're well paid,' said the Caretaker. 'Well paid indeed. Very well paid. — I used to tell them that labour was its own reward, but they couldn't understand that. They preferred payment, I discovered, and the better the pay the more work they did. Human nature has no secrets from me now.'

'What payment do they get?' asked Albyn.

'For everything they grow they receive one and a half times the price they would have got in my father's day. And in addition — in addition, mark you — the state gives them a grant amounting to half the price of their crop as a reward for having grown it.'

'How can the state afford to do that?'

'Two years ago,' said Od McGammon, 'I imposed a head-tax; and last year I doubled it. The art of government is very simple, if you have sufficient control. Very simple indeed — but you must have control. However, I didn't bring you here to talk statecraft. — I've been thinking that it would be a good plan to visit Furbister; and I want you to advise me about my journey.'

CHAPTER SEVENTEEN

'WHAT he's really going for,' said Albyn, 'is to see Bala. He's hugged my picture of her to his imagination, and rubbed it till it's raw. Now nothing will soothe it but a sight of her — and to see her may make him hotter still. There's the danger.'

'You made that danger,' said Liss. 'You talked of Bala, you inflamed him. And now, if he wants her and tries to take her from Furbister, there may indeed be war between Galloway and Carrick. A war for Bala!'

'How frightened and how happy it would make her. She'd howl the skies down, and shine through them like a rick on fire.'

'We can go home now, can't we? There's no purpose in staying longer here.'

'I am going tomorrow,' said Albyn reluctantly. 'I must warn Furbister — '

'You are going? Alone?'

'For a little while, for a few days only, I hope.'

'And I must stay here in Carrick?' cried Liss.

'That's his demand,' said Albyn miserably.

'But why, why?'

'Carrick won't trust in Galloway's good faith. His first intention was to meet Furbister with an army behind him: that would mean war at once. He must go alone, I told him; or, at the most, with two or three followers. "I may be murdered," he said, quite simply, like a man who knows how easy murder is. — "I'll tell Furbister," I said, "that you're coming to promise peace." — "When I'm asleep," he answered, "Furbister may see a short cut to peace." — Under his skin he's frightened. This afternoon he kept harping on Furbister's size and strength. Could he pull a tree out from the roots, and so forth. I could have told him that Furbister's more frightened by far of him. — But that's how it was, and safety was his other theme: he must see Bala, and equally must run no risk of being murdered. And then he thought of hostages.'

'The children and myself,' said Liss. 'My father, too, I suppose?'

Albyn knelt and hid his face in her lap. 'I've been a fool,' he cried, and his voice broke. 'A fool, and folly's never private to the fool; for all his household feels the whip.'

'You've been too clever,' said Liss. 'You may be too much of a poet or too little of a husband; I don't know. But my father distrusted you, and he was right. I thought a good lover would make a good husband, and I was wrong. You deceive me in Galloway, and in Carrick you abandon me; and if I were to fall out of love with you, I could say hard things about you.'

'Say what you like, I've no defence.'

'Poor fool,' said Liss, and stroked his hair. 'If you bring Od McGammon safely back, I suppose he will let us go?'

'He promised that. He swore it, most solemnly.'

'Do you trust him?'

'I would have done — in such a matter — two days ago. But now I've swung too far to your side, to hatred, to have any judgment left. — For you were right, do you see? and I was wrong to laugh instead of loathe. But I've learnt my lesson, and I'll do something yet on your side of belief. I'll think of something, I'll outwit him — '

'Don't boast about it now. Boast afterwards, if you like. Come now and see the children.'

'They'll grow up more yours than mine, I hope.'

'I hope so too, and yet they'll be the better of your blood. My father married his cousin, and if I had married one of mine, they would be very dull.'

'I thought,' said Albyn, 'that I could not love you more. That was another mistake I made.'

'I used to think,' said Liss, 'that I could never love a man who had failed me. I was wrong too.'

'Let me be humble, let me be humble, grateful and humble,' cried Albyn to the wind as he cantered southward on the road to Galloway. 'Never again, never again, shall I caper and strut and be clever. Never again to spin words like a noose, but save all the bright ones for Liss, a garland for Liss. No laughter, no ribaldry, only devotion. Love and devotion . . . Or is that,' he thought, pulling his pony to a walk, 'going too far?'

Sweating a furlong behind came a brace of soldiers whom Od McGammon had ordered to escort him to the frontier; but Albyn was scarcely aware of them. All his thoughts were of Liss, and love so disabled his vision that he saw nothing of any meaning in Od McGammon's kingdom, nothing of its strange economy, until evening flushed the fields and at the gable-end of a cottage his distant mind perceived a woman knitting, warm in the westering sun, and with a foot as busy as her fingers rocking a wooden cradle. There he halted, and sat for several minutes doting on motherhood, and quietude, and life made purposeful and more intense by love that closed it in. Tears blurred his sight; but surely, he thought, they magnified his understanding? — He rode on, slowly at first, then kicking his pony to a gallop, and was fiercely resolved that all his life henceforth would be in service to his perfect wife and a domestic love.

He wasted little time on sleep, and when they came to the frontier Od McGammon's soldiers were haggard and exhausted. Albyn went on alone — his pony, rack-ribbed and black with sweat, had a stubborn strength — and news of his return brought Furbister from his supper-table to greet him.

Furbister came out of his palace, jovial, and wiping his great mouth. He was not drunk, but had half a kilderkin of ale in him. He stooped, and taking Albyn under the armpits — his fingers meeting on the poet's backbone — lifted him to eye-level, and breathed on him like brewing-day. 'Welcome to my ambassador!' he cried. 'Did you steal a promise of peace from Carrick?'

'Carrick will tell you that himself,' said Albyn. 'He's on his way here, and will arrive, I think, the day after tomorrow.'

Furbister's taut look of geniality grew soft and foolish, his nerveless fingers lost their grip, and Albyn — clutching a thumb to break his fall — fell heavily to the turf. Furbister looked down at him, sprawling and irate, and said stupidly, 'Od McGammon coming here?'

Albyn rubbed a twisted ankle and replied, 'To talk of peace.'

Furbister, swaying a little, mumbled too deep in his

throat for understanding, then sat upon the grass and leaned his enormous back against the palace wall. 'Tell me the whole story,' he commanded.

His head was drooping when he had heard the end of it, and Albyn thought that drink had overcome him. But after a little while Furbister said, plainly enough, 'Wait here, and I shall bring Bala. There are too many in the hall, and I want no one else to hear.'

He rose heavily, stumbling as if his legs were cramped, and went into the palace. A few minutes later Bala came out with a comb of honey in one hand and a shallow bowl in the other. Sucking the comb, she held the bowl under her sticky chin to catch the drops, and before she spoke she licked her shining lips with her great scarlet tongue. 'What have you been telling Furbister,' she asked, 'to upset him so?'

Furbister followed her, grey-faced and loosely enormous beside her vast exuberance, and without raising his head sat down, once more, against the gable wall. Bala, folding her ponderous legs beneath a skirt that hung like a chequered tent from the belt below her portentous bosom, squatted beside him and with a commanding note of interrogation — honey dripping from her chin — cried, 'Well?'

A little mechanically, Albyn repeated his story, and for his private interest counted the differences between the Bala who sat before him, and the gigantic eager girl whom he had brought into Galloway two years before. — Her waist was thicker, her arms heavier, her shoulders fatter, her feet softer; there was a wrinkle in her neck, her cheeks were rounder, her voice harder, and her eyes were boldly confident. 'How big is Od McGammon?' she inquired.

'I told him,' said Albyn, 'that Furbister's the taller by two or three hands. But the truth is that there's very little difference between them.'

'It will be a pleasure,' she said, 'to see another man of proper height and build.'

'He means my death,' said Furbister, staring with wild eyes at his imagined doom.

'Oh, what nonsense,' said Bala. 'That's no way to speak about a visitor.'

'Do you not know,' cried Furbister in a voice of agony, 'that when giant sits down with giant there's always another waiting at the door? There's death on the threshold! And if Carrick comes to Galloway it's to bring death to Galloway — but I'm not ready, not ready yet, to meet him!'

'I'll be with you,' said Bala comfortably. 'There's no need to be frightened.' — And turning to Furbister she gave him a great honey-sweet kiss.

'I'm not ready for him yet,' groaned Furbister. 'Another year — let me have another year — and I could deal with him.'

'We have another day,' said Albyn thoughtfully.

'Furbister can stay in bed,' said Bala. 'If he doesn't want to meet Od McGammon, there's no reason why he should. I'll say he's ill.'

'That's well thought of,' said Albyn. 'It's very well thought of. And I do believe I can think it into an even better shape!'

CHAPTER EIGHTEEN

FURBISTER gave them no help on the following day, for his immediate assumption — on hearing of Od McGammon's unsolicited visit — that Od McGammon could have no purpose but his murder, had quite unnerved him. Bala, to begin with, was openly and vainly gratified by the prospect of entertaining the Caretaker, not with her husband's state, but by her own merit; and Albyn had to argue for two solid hours before she would believe that Carrick, so far from being merely an interesting visitor, was a menace to Galloway and a serious threat to her own well-being. But though she was hard to convince, she was whole-hearted as anyone could wish when understanding had finally penetrated the gross ramparts of flesh and bone that enclosed her small intelligence; and a little while later, with a deep gurgle of laughter like the ebb-tide emptying a cleft in the rocks, she was loudly applauding the device that Albyn proposed for the discomfiture of Od McGammon.

She would certainly, she promised, persuade Furbister to play his necessary part; and in a gust of simple enjoyment, and with the unpremeditated affection of an ingenuous nature frankly pleased, she seized Albyn by his left shoulder and right buttock and pressed him to her bosom. He was almost stifled in the deep profundity between her breasts, that first impended, then closed upon him like Atlantic billows on a shallow reef; and only by kicking furiously at her midriff was he able to escape from suffocation.

She set him on her right knee and said admiringly, 'What a good little poet you are, to think of a plan like that!'

Albyn, somewhat pale and still short of breath, had sufficient command of his wits to reply, 'It was you who gave me the first inkling of it. You and a woman on the Carrick side of the frontier, who was rocking her child and spinning in the sun. And then I saw a boat on the shore, not far from here. A big well-built boat with a keel of sixteen feet or so. You must have it brought to the palace, and we'll need some timber, and a couple of carpenters. And all the people, as many as you can warn, must be ordered to line the roads and greet Od McGammon when he comes; and wait for his return.'

Happy beyond measure at being entrusted with so much that was important, Bala assured him that everything would be done exactly to his wishes, and having embraced him once more — to the great peril of his ribs — she went into the palace to prepare Furbister, sweating on a couch, for his share in the reception.

It was late in the afternoon, on the next day, when Albyn led Od McGammon into Wigtown. Attended by a troop of Furbister's cavalry he had met the Caretaker some fifteen miles beyond the town, and sworn to him on the security of Liss and their children that there was no plot against his life nor any design upon his safety. Od McGammon, pale and serious and splendidly attired in a saffron shirt and a new-woven plaid of harebell-blue and russet checks, had stared at him with searching gaze and grimly said, 'I trust you — because I must!'

'Not altogether,' Albyn replied, looking at the forty horsemen who accompanied the giant.

'They are for politeness' sake,' said Od McGammon. 'For ceremony only. Just for ceremony.'

'They're well-dressed,' said Albyn. 'They'll please Bala. Bala's fond of gay colours; of all gaiety, indeed. She likes tall men and a brave approach.'

They rode swiftly down to Wigtown, Od McGammon striding in their midst with Albyn at his side.

'Has she much influence in the kingdom?' he inquired.

'At present, she's the regent,' said Albyn. 'Furbister has gone to visit friends in Cumberland. We expect him back within a day or two.'

'So when I arrive,' said Od McGammon, 'I'll be received by Bala? By Bala, eh? She'll be my hostess, she alone? Charged with the task of entertainment, eh? There'll be no one else to whom I must pay court?'

'No one,' said Albyn. 'No one but Bala till Furbister comes wading home from Cumberland across the Solway Firth.'

'That broad sea, in front of us? It's too deep for wading.'

'Too deep for most of us; but Furbister goes out in the morning to blow his nose upon the tree-tops.'

'Is it true, then, that he's taller than I?'

'I told you so in Carrick.'

'But Bala's not so high?'

'A good height. You couldn't say she's small.'

'If you measured her against me —'

'She would make a good match for you,' said Albyn.

'What a fine country you have here, on the southern side of the hills!' exclaimed Od McGammon. 'A fine country. How rich and open it lies to the sun! Not cultivated as it should be — you don't work as we in Carrick do — but spacious, handsome and spacious. Bala has brown hair, you said?'

Albyn, yet again, discussed the opulence of Bala's colour, liveliness, and figure; and Od McGammon, his solemn lineaments dissolving to enormous wistfulness — he mopped his brow, and said the sun felt warmer here — marched down to Wigtown amid the clatter of ponies' hooves, surrounded by flies, and enclosed in a sweet warmth of horse-flesh and grassy dung.

A mile from the town they met the outermost groups of those who had been commanded to greet their distinguished visitor; and Albyn quickly saw that Bala had been both energetic and efficient. The people who lined the road were in their best clothes, they appeared to be gay, and there were enough of them to suggest a populous and thriving country. Here were pipers and flute-players, there were children dancing, and young women to throw flowers. In the streets of Wigtown there was such a crowd, all clad in chequered clothes of green and yellow — the men in belted plaids, some holly-dark with primrose lines, some pale as opening beech-leaves criss-crossed with broom; and the women in grass-green frocks and woollen shawls the hue of king-cups — that the town looked like spring itself, flaunting its new growth; and harpers plucked their strings, whose notes came shining through the general shout of welcome. Od McGammon looked left and right, a little flustered, being unused to gaiety; and when they came to the precincts of Furbister's palace, and Albyn said that his escort of Carrick troopers must stay outside, he made no demur, but strode on alone.

Under the gable-end of the palace, warm in the westering sun, they saw Bala, huge and placid, spinning in a golden light, while with one enormous foot she rocked a gigantic cradle. It was a cradle as big as a sea-going boat — a boat whose keel might be sixteen feet long, or so — but its sides were draped with white woollen cloth, a canopy gave shadow to its head, and it stood on heavy rockers that let Bala swing it from side to side in a ponderous, creaking rhythm. 'Hush ye, hush ye, little pet ye,' she sang in a dreadful aggravation of mother-love; 'Od McGammon shall not get thee!'

'Who is that?' asked Od McGammon.

'Bala,' said Albyn.

'But in the cradle?'

'Her child. Didn't I tell you she had a child?'

'No!'

'He's six months old, and remarkably well-grown for his age. Come and look at him.'

Doubtfully, fearfully, Od McGammon approached the cradle, and Bala, with an exclamation of well-affected surprise, got up and came towards him. Like a landslide she curtsied, and rising like a forest-fire — for her face was scarlet with excitement — she cried, 'Welcome to Galloway, Your Majesty! Your dear, enormous Majesty!'

Od McGammon swayed upon his heels, his mouth gaped open. Enraptured by the preposterous extent of Bala's turgid beauty, his senses swam; but he was terrified by the apparent size of her six-months babe. He bent above the cradle, looked in, and saw beneath the blankets a gigantic shape, as large as himself, and beneath a ribboned cap a huge pale face and great harsh features. The infant's cheeks were rough as sail-cloth, and its eyelids, rising, disclosed eyes as big as a goose-egg and bloodshot to the rim.

'He takes after his father,' said Bala modestly. 'His father is very big. He can hold me in the palm of his hand, as if I were a child.'

'Furbister, you said,' cried Od McGammon to Albyn, 'was taller than I by two or three hands. No more than that, you said. Two hands, or two and a half!'

'Two *times*, I said, or two and a half times,' Albyn answered. 'Here's Furbister's son, already as tall as you at six months old; and Furbister himself — well, you will see, as soon as he comes home.'

The day was still and sultry. Beneath a sun that seemed to be melting like butter in its own heat the land lay drowsily in a golden light; but in the south-west, low beyond a rim of snowy cloud, the sky was purpled by a quickly moving thunderstorm that had come from Ireland. — Tormented by desire when he looked at the unfathomable extent of Bala's beauty, but racked with fear when he thought of the immeasurable sire who had begotten this inordinate child, Od McGammon stood with twisted hands and a grimace of piteous indecision above the cradle. Precursor of the storm, a little breeze fluttered Bala's clothing, pressing it more closely to the profundity between her breasts, more closely to the rolling acreage of her hips. She turned her scarlet face to snuff the wind, and the movement enlivened all her mighty parts. Od McGammon's breath came whistling through his nostrils, and almost he resolved to stay and dare his rival giant. But at that moment they heard the first rumble of the storm, and Albyn, in a casual voice, inquired, 'Is that Furbister?'

'It's thunder,' said simple Bala.

'I thought it might be Furbister. He had a cough when I last saw him.'

Od McGammon, credulous but unwilling to admit belief — appetent but unmanned by fear — glanced at the coming storm and stared at Bala with a devouring gaze. Then, as though to examine the evidence for Furbister's surpassing magnitude, he bent again above the sixteen-foot cradle, and with his enormous fore-finger stirred the bedclothes gathered about the neck of its long occupant. And as he leaned and fumbled, the thunder, in a nearer crack, more loudly roared.

'Furbister, I think,' said Albyn; and Od McGam-mon let out a bellow of pain.

In the cradle, wrapt round in blankets so tightly that he could shift neither hand nor foot, Furbister had lain as fearful and bemused as Od McGammon bending over him. Only an image of Furbister daunted Od McGammon's apprehension, but for Furbister it was Od McGammon himself who darkened the sky — and when he saw a great gnarled finger, tipped with a nail like a peat-cutter's spade, come poking at his neck, he snapped and bit it to the bone.

Od McGammon howled in agony, and above the cradle the air was infected by a preternatural stink. — Perhaps a thunderbolt had fallen nearby, and spread a sulphurous mist. — Furbister unclenched his teeth, and raised his voice in an earsplitting bay of alarm. Od McGammon waved a bloody finger in the air, whim-pered like a pack of hounds, and turning on his enormous heels fled from the palace with ungainly speed.

Thunder crackled and roared again; and Bala's high-pitched laughter brought down a splashing rain. Furbister in his cradle struggled to sit up, and having made sure that the Caretaker was gone, bounced with glee. Lightning slashed the sky.

Heedless of the jeering crowds who waited for him in the streets — deaf to the scornful music of the pipers and blind to the laughing girls who stood in the rain and pelted him with wet nosegays — Od McGammon ran headlong out of Wigtown, headlong to the north.

CHAPTER NINETEEN

SOME half a dozen people were kicked or trampled to death by Od McGammon in his panic-stricken flight, but only their nearest relatives stopped to mourn for them; for the majority considered that so small a loss was an easy price to pay for their riddance of the Carrick giant. His bodyguard, ashamed and discredited, followed and found him sitting on a peat-bank a mile beyond the frontier, miserably looking to the south, and brooding over the scene of his defeat. Albyn, on a sweating pony, arrived an hour or two later; he felt uneasy about his reception, but he had to return to Carrick to bring home Liss and their children and King Glam.

Od McGammon seemed not to notice him. So dull, disconsolate, and woebegone was the giant that for a day and a night he sat speechless on the peat-bank, hardly moving, while his bodyguard grumbled softly and awaited his pleasure. Then, still without speaking, and clumsy as a sleep-walker, he rose and marched sullenly back to his own kingdom.

Not until they were in sight of Ayr did he pay any attention to Albyn, but a mile from the town, at the edge of a little wood, he called him and bade him sit down; and told the captain of his bodyguard to ride on.

'I have been examining my soul and conscience,' said the giant, and lowered his great bulk to a soft slope, brown with pine-needles, beside Albyn. 'To judge by results — and what else can you judge by? — there's a flaw in my nature. An unsuspected flaw. I was discomfited in Wigtown, not by a major force, but by the failure of my own confidence. I went in peace, and I had nothing to fear from Furbister, however big he is. However big! But I was betrayed by some weakness in myself, a weakness I had never guessed, and that even now I cannot name. What is my weakness, Albyn?'

To Albyn it seemed clear enough that Od McGammon had run away for the best and simplest of reasons: because he was frightened to stay. But he could not put it so bluntly as that, and before he could think of a more tactful explanation, Od McGammon had resumed his self-examination.

'I'm not like other men,' he said. 'Not like other men at all. No, not at all! My personality's more complicated than yours, for example. Also — and this is a practical consideration, so I hope you won't be offended — also, of course, I'm infinitely more important. I am not only Od McGammon, I am Carrick. I am the state, and the state is me. I made it! And therefore, if there is a weakness in me, it may be part and parcel of a weakness in my people. There may be some fault in the relationship between us — '

'Do you love them?' asked Albyn.

'Love them?' demanded the giant, quacking like an old drake in a summer storm. 'Of course not! Why should I? Do you love people?'

'I get on with them well enough, but my wife says I should do more than that. We fell out the other day, and she found a fault in me. A bad fault, she said. It was lack of love.'

'I don't understand! I don't understand that at all. My Carrick herds — the two-legged cattle of the country — are by nature idle, vain, dissolute, and dishonest. Sluggards unless they're greedy, and all who aren't too dull of wit will cheat you if they're able! You can't trust them out of sight, and what pleasure do you get when you look at them? Their minds are feeble, and their bodies frail. They're helpless in childhood, a nuisance in old age, and their middle life they spend whoring and breeding, filling their bellies and emptying them, arguing over flies, quarrelling about shadows, and drinking to forget their nullity. — Why should I love them? There's no reason under the sun. But I do better, I make use of them! Those that can dig, must dig, and fishermen must go to sea. Women bear children, blacksmiths must stick to the anvil, and my officers command obedience from each and see that each in his degree and according to capacity contributes to the whole. A man is nothing, a woman rather less. But organize and set them all to work, prescribe their tasks and see they're fulfilled before the cattle eat — why, then you can make something of humanity, and every sly, dull, crippled piece of it can serve a purpose. I make use of people, I take care of them. I feed and shelter them to preserve their usefulness — but why should I love them?'

'Perhaps you cannot argue about it,' said Albyn. 'Perhaps love is a gift. My wife has it.'

'So have my cattle, in a way,' said Od McGammon. 'They get frantic about each other from time to time —'

'No, no! It's not that at all. It's quite, quite different. This sort of love, that my wife has, doesn't seem to be selective. Or, if it does select, it chooses the very people that your sort has overlooked, or finished and done with, or despised.'

'And what benefit does your wife get? What's her return?'

'I don't know,' said Albyn. 'So far as I can see, she gets nothing. It's an unselfish love.'

'You're not putting up a very good case for it.'

'I wish,' said Albyn, 'that I could remember a story I heard when I went into Northumbria to bring Bala home. There were some soldiers in her village, deserters from the Roman army that has conquered, so they say, the south of Britain, and is now fighting for more territory in the middle parts of England.'

'Are they good soldiers, these Romans?' asked Od McGammon.

'They have conquered about as much of the earth as would make another moon, if it could be cut away and thrown into the sky.'

'I'm not frightened of them,' said Od McGammon. 'No Roman army will enter Carrick while I'm alive. Not while I'm alive!'

'I'm sure I hope not,' said Albyn. 'But I, being a poet, was more interested to hear what sort of men they were, who lived within the empire, than in the boundaries of their empire. And one of the soldiers, a Syrian, told me a story —'

'About love?' asked Od McGammon.

'I can't remember. It's only the beginning of the story that sticks in my mind, for it began with the sort of difficulty that you're in now. — There were three kings who ruled over great territories and a numerous people. They were grave men, grave and good, who had given all their genius and care to the conduct and government of their kingdoms; and every year they used to meet, in one or other of their capital cities, to compare and discuss the measures they had taken for the improvement of their states, and to boast a little, I suppose, about their new roads and good harvests.'

'Who were these kings?' asked Od McGammon.

'One was called Melchior, another was King Jaspar of Taurus, and the third — no, I've forgotten. But the point of the story is that they were all dissatisfied. Year after year their kingdoms became richer and more orderly, their subjects were prosperous and well-behaved and worked harder than ever before; but in spite of uncountable improvements in their life, no one seemed any happier. They complained, indeed, of the dullness of their life, and the women went so far as to say that if it weren't for foreign visitors they might as well be dead. — Now the three kings were deeply concerned about the failure of their plans and the defeat of their good intentions. They were the more deeply concerned because they themselves were growing weary of endeavour that now seemed to have no purpose, and they took less and less pleasure in the crowded busy streets of their capital cities. "It seems to me," said one of them — it may have been Melchior — "that when we cast out the bloody-minded gods our people used to worship, and banished all fear of the doom their gods had threatened, we also threw away the warmth and glee with which they had been worshipped. What we need, perhaps, is a new god."

'"Then we had better follow the new star that my magicians have been watching," said another of the kings — Jaspar of Taurus, I think — "for they tell me that it heralds the birth of a prophet, or a king, or a god perhaps, who shall unlock the secret of the universe: which is the secret, I take it, of man's purpose upon earth, and how he should be ruled. Let us follow the star and find what it foretells."

'So the kings, being good men and tormented by desire of virtue, decided to follow the star; and disguising themselves as soothsayers, they called their servants to bring their boots, and set out on their journey. They had a hard time of it, for it was winter and the passes were choked with snow; but they were men of great fortitude, and neither the cold nor the wolves howling in the darkness could halt or dismay them. One was called Melchior, another was King Jaspar of Taurus, and the third — was his name Balthasar?'

'But what did they find?' asked Od McGammon.

'That,' said Albyn, 'is what I don't know. I may have forgotten, or perhaps I was never told. It was the Syrian deserter's story, and the others made a butt of him. He knew a lot of stories — he was a talkative fellow — and sometimes the others laughed at him and encouraged him, but sometimes they got impatient and wouldn't let him go on. Perhaps he never finished the story. I liked him well enough, but he must have been the poorest soldier Rome ever had.'

'How did he come to be in the army?'

'He had been caught in some conscription, and trained, and sent to England; and the first chance he had, he deserted. He had joined some small religious sect, just before the army took him, and he didn't believe in fighting. He believed that a man should love his neighbours — all of them — just as deeply as he loved himself. The others took advantage of him, of course, but he was very good-natured. There was no wisdom but love, he used to say, and nothing availed that was not done in love.'

'You mean, of course, the other sort of love? Not the sort that befools my two-legged cattle?'

'No, not that sort.'

'And you don't know what happened to the three kings? Did they go back to their kingdoms?'

'I'm inclined to think,' said Albyn, 'that the story was never finished. I believe I'd have remembered it, if it had been.'

'And you can't explain to me what this other sort of love really is? How you put it into practice, and how it works? How it works, eh? That's what I want to know.'

'As I said before, it may be a gift — and either you have it or you haven't, and you can't argue about it.'

'You're not as helpful as I had hoped you would be,' said Od McGammon. 'But I'll think about what you've said — though I don't like the idea! I tell you plainly, I don't like it at all!'

CHAPTER TWENTY

ON the shore not far from Od McGammon's
palace there was a small bay, no bigger than a
paddock, within two horns of shelving rock.
The trees grew so close to the water's edge that at
high tide, on a calm clear morning, their topmost
branches were reflected, a deeper green, in the pale
green sea; and rooks flew out and gulls flew in to make
a chequered pattern of black and white. It was here
that Od McGammon had discussed with Albyn his
visit to Wigtown; and here the giant, who was much
given to solitude and immobility, used often to come
and meditate on the affairs of his kingdom. — On the
night of his return from Galloway, as soon as he had
had his supper, he went down to the little bay to
ponder Albyn's unfinished story, and the utility of
love.

He was utterly perplexed by the nature of spiritual
love, and found it very difficult to think about. Of
carnal love he had seen enough to be disgusted by it
in youth, and extremely bored in later years. He had
no practical experience of it, and since the disaster of
his visit to Wigtown he had been deeply ashamed of
the excitement that Bala had roused in his hitherto
reasonable mind. Never again, he decided, would he
waste a thought on her or any other giantess. — But
carnal love, he realized, was not the problem. The
business of loving a whole people, of loving even
twenty people, was clearly very different from that
heat and turmoil of the blood which so betrayed

humanity two by two; and yet was so curiously esteemed by human kind. How could a larger but less vulgar love be created, or procured? And what was it like? What were its sensations? Of what did it consist? How should it be 'declared, and what were its proper actions?

Motionless among the trees, Od McGammon sat throughout the summer night — the air was warm and still — and canvassed the mystery that, to Albyn's wife and a Syrian deserter, it seemed, was no mystery at all. He thought of the three kings and their winter journey, and wondered what they had found and how their kingdoms had profited. — But he found no answer to his questions, and exhausted by his efforts to understand what he had never known, he fell asleep before dawn; and slept where he sat, head sunk upon his chest, like a cairn of stones among the trees.

He woke again when the sun came through the branches and warmed his shoulders; and raising his head, looked dully at the leaf-green sea. Then, jaw tightening, brows contracting, he stared and glared upon a scene of utter shamelessness.

Naked on the beach, lying in close embrace upon the clothes which they had doffed to make a couch, a man and a young woman lay fast asleep. Her yellow head was pillowed on his arm, her arm enclasped his shoulder, and his red hair, flaming in the sun, threw a bronze light on hers. Her waist, beneath his hand, was small and shallow above the fullness of her hips, and her back was so flexible that everywhere she pressed close against his sturdier and less yielding body. — So trim and compact was the picture they presented that, for two or three minutes, Od McGammon was disarmed of anger; and perceived what was more remarkable than the affection which held them so close. How astonishing was the human ability to make — with a digestive trunk, a cumbrous bony head, and two pragmatic pairs of unequal limbs — a pattern so conformable to mutual desire, and pleasing to the aesthetic eye! For a few philosophic moments the giant admitted that aspect of their shame, and was hindered in his moral judgment, and prevented from outspoken wrath. And in that interval the sleepers woke.

She stirred, and turned her head. Jealous of comfort, he moved the closer; but she pushed him off, sat up, and yawned. He roused and blinked, and looked at her reproachfully. She bent above him, pouted a kiss; and wrestling with his hands, stood up and freed herself. He tried to grasp her by the ankle, and pull her down again, but she eluded him, and mocked him, and without looking back ran down into the sea. Grumbling and moving slowly as a bear, he followed to the water's edge, then leapt across a little crumbling wave, and with threshing arms swam outward in pursuit.

She waited for him, treading water, and face to face in fathom depth they kissed. Then purposeful, with steady strokes, they swam to sea, and when their heads were small in the rising sun they turned to shore again, and in shallower water grew playful, dived and ducked each other, shouting, and splashing with their hands. They came ashore, and hand in hand walked up the little beach. They sat upon their heels, as close as knee to knee, and looked upon each other with adoring eyes, and talked in unheard voices.

Dry-mouthed and taut with anger, Od McGammon

lay flat upon his monstrous belly, concealing himself as best he could among the pine trees, and watched with mounting fury this spectacle of a love that had no use in statecraft. — True, they were married, the two participants, for as soon as they roused he had recognized Liss and Albyn. But did not their marriage make the exhibition more reprehensible? For marriage was supposed to subdue the flesh, but Albyn and his princess, so far from being sobered by familiarity and their vows, appeared to have nourished their temper on permission and to be warmer by far than untried colts and fillies tentative of the game. — 'Carnal and unashamed! Oh, gross carnality!' quacked Od Mc-Gammon, pressing down against the pine needles and cursing his remembrance of Bala and the excitement she had roused. 'How can I love humanity when human kind is but a set of sensual clowns?'

And then a more bitter thought occurred to him, for Albyn had talked of a love that transcended mere desire, but what Albyn practised was the common love that falsified all reason and sank the small precarious judgment of mankind in the common flux of appetite. Albyn had mocked him! Albyn, debating with apparent gravity the fearful problems of the world, had been hiding in his heart his secret thoughts of common joy!

Albyn had mocked him, Albyn had perplexed him with talk of an absolute love that might change the universe, but Albyn sprawling on the sand had shown him such a scene of love as made him common flesh with swineherds, old rams in autumn, and sparrows pecking at the dung. Love was no cleansing, healing thing, but common drunkenness.

Afraid to speak, lest anger should break his voice

and make a mocking turmoil of his words, Od McGammon shifted his great bulk, in clumsy motion, farther from the beach; and lay hidden in a dell till he grew calm again. When at last he rose, he found that Liss and Albyn had dressed themselves and gone.

He had no wish to see them again. He returned to his palace and gave orders that they and the King must remove themselves at once. They must be on their way by noon, he said, and to let them out of his thoughts as soon as possible, he made no demur when Liss demanded leave to take her nurses, the milkmaid, and her cow as well. But to King Glam's request that the soldiers and the pioneers and priests who had come in with them should also be released, Od McGammon said no. They had been put to work, and they were useful to him.

At noon, then, King Glam and his diminished retinue set out on their road; and two days later Od McGammon followed to see if they were still within his territory. — He saw them, moving slowly, a little party in a wide and empty countryside, and climbing to a hill-top he looked down to where Galloway lay like a golden shadow against the misty sea. And hatred, like rats coming out of a drain, came out of the darkness of his mind and devoured him.

Down there lay Furbister, a giant greater than he, and the warm amplitude of Bala was his comfort and his plaything. Galloway faced the south, and life was easier there. The soil was rich and profligate, like his father's court; and there too they had laughed at him. Laughter had beaten on his ears when he ran from Wigtown, smacking his face with its horny din. Laughter like the coarse voices that beat above his father's table, fanned by the gusty words of men with red faces who enjoyed the world they lived in. — How he had hated their laughter and enjoyment, and his father who ruled the rich, untidy board at which they drank! And now, like an echo of his father's court, he remembered the mocking crowds in the streets of Wigtown; and in the arms of the giant who ruled the land lay Bala, that ponderous enchantment, as many a strange woman had lain in his father's arms.

It was by a curious chance that while Od McGammon was looking down from the hills and hating Galloway and his dead father, Furbister was looking up at the hills and hating Carrick and his dead mother. Furbister, of course, could not remember that his mother's breasts had been insufficient for his infant greed, but he remembered very well his resentment against her. She had denied him something, or everything perhaps, and she remained in his memory as a symbol of denial. And now the hills above him, and the land of Carrick beyond them, stood also for denial. For he wanted power, and he wanted peace if it could be dictated by his power; but Carrick prevented his desire. The shape of the hills was hard and fruitless, and in his infancy he had beaten his head against barren slopes. Why could he never get all he wanted? Why, when he so hated his mother, had he been frightened of her? And why was he still frightened of Od McGammon, after Od McGammon had run away from him?

Albyn, had he known of it, would have been delighted by the picture of the two giants, with only a day's journey between them, hating each other because the one had hated his mother, the other his father. But Albyn, with his elder child in his arms, was plodding in the dust, while the younger of the two nurses, who had blistered her heel, rode his pony. In Albyn's heart there was nothing that bore the smallest likeness to hatred; but as the child grew heavier in his arms, and Liss complained that he was not carrying her properly, the thought occurred to him that a little while ago, in a warm flush of remorse and gratitude and love, he had perhaps over-rated the happiness of domestic love.

CHAPTER TWENTY-ONE

AS soon as the harvest was in, Furbister led an army to the east and quickly subdued the several small clans in the valleys of the Annan and the Esk which, as he had long maintained, were a menace to the peace of his realm.

He put away the sloth, and ease, and relative geniality that, in the first two years of his married life, had made life tolerable in Galloway; and grew urgent, harsh, and imperious. When winter set in and the people, as was their custom, took to lying long abed in the morning, and gathering in each other's houses in the early twilight to drink and make love in the lazy hours of darkness — or to sing, and hear stories, and dance to the music of bapgipe and flute — Furbister turned them out at sunrise and moon-up to practise with their weapons and learn military drill. Winter was their time of holiday, after the sweat of harvest and the killing and the salting of their young beasts, for which there was no winter fodder: it was their season of rest and jollity, before the earth should wake again and call them out to the stern labours of ploughing, and fishing in yet stormy seas, and peat-cutting in the wet hills, and mending the roofs that winter gales had weakened. — But Furbister changed all that. He and his officers went throughout the land making speeches that spoiled all the simple people's enjoyment of singing and dancing, of story-telling and making love, and even of drinking. The whole of Galloway, said Furbister and his officers, was in mortal danger; for Od

McGammon, with the power of Carrick behind him, was busily preparing to march in and lay it waste, and there was no defence against him but to create, before spring should come, a great army to march northward and strike before Carrick was ready.

Furbister's speeches on this subject were most effective. Sometimes, when he remembered how he had bitten Od McGammon's finger, and Od McGammon had howled and fled, he was extremely scornful of the Carrick giant, and boasted that it would be easy to conquer him. Sometimes, when he admitted to himself that, in spite of Od McGammon's discomfiture in Wigtown, he was still strangely frightened of him, he warned his audience that only by the sternest resolution and the utmost self-sacrifice could they hope to defeat the inhuman monster who ruled beyond the hills. But whatever his mood might be, his voice was always resonant with hatred, and all those who heard him — or nearly all — were excited by his passion and came to the sad conclusion that military drill was a more suitable occupation, for that winter at least, than dancing and singing and making love.

Among the exceptions were Albyn and Liss and the Oldest Druid; and of these three it was Liss who made the strongest, and certainly the most material protest against Furbister's preparations for the killing of many of his own subjects and, it was to be hoped, many more of Od McGammon's. A week before Yule she announced that about midsummer, or a little later, she would be having another baby.

Albyn showed less pleasure than she had expected. Despite his great love for Liss, and his growing fondness of the two children whom she had borne already, he sometimes, in the midst of his family, felt a recurrence of the fear that had assailed him in the broch, when Liss first showed that she had more than beauty to sustain her. For all its kindliness and genial warmth, a family was a sort of prison, a very strong and subtle prison, from which only a resolute and brutal person could break out. The prison-breaker must even be brutal to himself — for family life was more comfortable than any other — but there were times when Albyn remembered his colder and untrammelled years, the rough freedom of his youth, and wondered whether some day he might turn heartless enough to forsake his fireside bliss. He would wince and rebuke himself even as he thought of it; but the thought recurred. It re-entered his mind now, when Liss told him of his increasing fatherhood; for every child was another bolt on the prison-gate, and Ferli too would be adding to his score about the end of February. — A glimpse of freedom and the wisp of a thought about escape came in upon the heels of Liss's news; but promptly he smothered them with shame.

'You might,' he said, 'have chosen a more suitable time. Isn't it reckless to start breeding again when we're on the verge of what may be a disastrous war?'

'It's the very time to breed!' declared Liss in her most vigorous tones. 'When men call up death to help their policies, women must call up life to help their purpose. I've no faith in policies — for who can speak for a whole people? — but I know myself and believe in myself. There's far more knowledge of life in the little satchel of my womb than there is in Furbister's great barrel of a head!'

'But if the child's a man-child,' said Albyn, 'he'll

have the faults of men. He'll believe in policy — he may even invent a policy, and recruit a party — and so destroy the children of other women.'

'He may,' said Liss, 'but he may be more sensible. The day may come when even men have a little grace and a little sense. The world's still young, the Druids say, and the child in my womb will help it to grow up.'

'Your faith is stronger than mine,' said Albyn.

'Much,' agreed Liss.

'And in some ways your mind is more robust.'

'It needs to be,' she said.

'But I've a better mind! My mind's more subtle and more critical. You've faith, you say, but I wrestle with my thoughts. I want to find constructive thoughts, but you take what's given and are satisfied.'

'My womb constructs, and what it makes may live for sixty years. Will your thoughts last as long?'

'Why, God forbid!' said Albyn. 'I can grow tired of my thoughts in sixty minutes, and always in sixty days. — But while they last they're more attractive than any woman's nurseling!'

'Are you sure?' asked Liss. 'Come and look at your children.'

Before they could go to the children's chamber, however, the Oldest Druid came into the hall, and as soon as he was told that Liss was in the family way again, he grew very talkative and most benignly cheerful. For he never heard of a new-born babe, or a child remotely anticipated, but he thought of an innocent soul that might be won for God; and though in his long life he had had countless disappointments, his hope was still strong, and to young expectant mothers he was a very fountain of benevolence, and good advice, and forty years of gossip. But Albyn soon grew weary of his talk, and yawned till bed-time came.

Then, in the morning, he repented of his surliness, and decided that Liss was setting an example of gallantry and wisdom. 'Let us have seven children at least,' he said, clipping her in the warmth of their bed; and presently went out to mock at Furbister's soldiers drilling for death.

It was the custom throughout Galloway to feast for fourteen days in mid-winter, from three days before Yule till the third day after the New Year; but this year Furbister decreed two days only for the Yule feast, and two days to greet the New Year. The remaining days, he said, must be spent on military exercise.

So one afternoon, not long before the New Year, Albyn was watching the men of Wigtown drilling on a field that a light fall of snow had whitened, and he looked at the slingers hurling smooth pebbles from their slings, and the swordsmen charging, the spearmen standing well forward over their left knees to receive the charge; and he had to admit that they made a very handsome sight, for all were sturdy and most were young, and their bodies were taut, their faces ruddy with the exercise, and discipline had given to their movements a dignified but lively pattern. — If Furbister had a good cause, he thought, this would truly be a noble spectacle, in spite of what Liss believes. If these men were preparing to fight for their honour, and their wives and their fields, against some foreign invader, then their policy would deserve all praise and their exercise be as devout and splendid as a hymn. But as it is, of course, they're merely wasting their time as a preliminary to wasting their lives. For Furbister, whom I don't dislike, is in fact an overgrown fool, and Od McGammon, whom I detest, is just such another, only worse. If it hadn't been for their lamentable birth, neither Galloway nor Carrick would be in the smallest danger, or feel any temptation to go to war. — Do all rulers who have too much power bring misfortune on those they rule?

While he was considering this possibility, a cold flurry of snow hid from sight the men who were drilling, and their officers came to the conclusion that they might as well be dismissed. Then Albyn, talking to half a dozen whom he knew, found himself inviting twice that number to come and drink in his hall, and before they arrived the dozen had grown to a score. Liss and the Oldest Druid were talking by the fire when they went in, but Liss withdrew and sent in her maids with ale. The young soldiers drank thirstily, laughed heartily, and talked loudly of their exercise. They were not much concerned about the rights or wrongs of the war in which they would soon be engaged, but showed a cheerful pride in the accomplishment of their own troop of slingers, or swordsmen, or spearmen; and some propensity to cry down the skill of those in other troops. All, moreover, spoke well of Furbister, and put great trust in his surpassing height and the strength of his arms.

Albyn, going from one to the other and telling them not to stint themselves, listened to what they were saying, and was sorry for their lack of judgment. So he attracted general attention by exclaiming in a loud voice, 'Poor Furbister! How sorry I am for him! There's no unhappier man on earth, unless it's Od McGammon. I'm sorry for him too.'

The young men gathered round him, some laughing to pretend he had been joking; others, more serious, protesting that he could not mean what he said.

'I do indeed,' said Albyn, 'and I'm sorrier still for you. It's very dangerous for a man in Furbister's position to be unhappy. I would as soon have a criminal to rule over us.'

A thin-faced, black-browed, grave young soldier inquired, 'Do you mean that an unhappy man is no better than a criminal?'

'You can take your choice between them,' said Albyn with a shrug. 'For myself, I think a known criminal, an habitual criminal, is often less dangerous; for it's easier to guess what he will do.'

'What's this? What's this?' cried the Oldest Druid, pushing his way through the young men who surrounded Albyn. The young men, to be polite, had all been offering mugs of ale to the Oldest Druid, and the Druid, to prove he was as much a man as they, had drunk more than most of them. 'What's this you're saying about unhappiness?' he asked.

'That it's dangerous when it has authority,' said Albyn. 'You know our custom with an idiot child: we take him to the sea, and drown him as quickly and kindly as we can. You know what we do with a grown man who goes mad: we stone him to death. And why? Because the idiot child, if he grew up, would breed more idiots; and the madman, if he ran free, might set our roofs on fire. — And how does the unhappy man behave? He wants revenge for his unhappiness, and either he seeks power to get revenge, or makes a mock of life to spread his own dissatisfaction. And so, perhaps — '

But the young man with the black brows who had interrupted Albyn before, now interrupted him again, and said, 'Many of our best story-tellers, many of our greatest musicians, were unhappy men; and out of their unhappiness they made some of our finest tales and favourite songs.'

Swaying slightly on his heels, but speaking most solemnly, the Oldest Druid said: 'We're indebted to unhappy men for many of our most inspiring hymns. Religion would never survive without unhappiness. You have naughty ideas, Albyn, very naughty ideas, and if ever you try to rule Galloway, I'll excommunicate you!'

'Have no fear of that,' said Albyn. 'I am a poet, and content to be what I am. I tell you what I think to stir your thoughts, not to compel them; and some of my thoughts are good, though they've no authority, and one of the best I've ever had is that we've drunk enough ale, and now we'd all be the better of a little mead. — Find my butler,' he said to the grave young man with black brows, 'and tell him to bring some of the four-year-old from the inner cellar.'

The grave young man did as he was told, and the mead went round and round again, and revived the Yule-tide gaiety that Albyn's theories had quietened a little.

'I must tell you,' said Albyn, taking the floor again, 'that I have been having a solemn argument with my wife, who believes that whenever Furbister goes out to war, the women should stay at home to breed. And our argument reminded me of a song my mother used to sing in my boyhood, when we travelled from shore to shore, all across the borderlands of England and Scotland. It's a song she learnt in England, it was made by a blind man in Otterburn, in Northumberland, out of a story they've long told in Northumberland of two old men, who were brothers, and went about the country daunting everyone with the great cudgels they carried.

'One of the old men would hit out at anyone he met, man, woman, or child, and such was the weight of his stick that every blow meant death, whether it fell on head or shoulder, ribs or shins. But the other old man beat only women or well-grown girls, and as soon as he'd belaboured them they laughed and grew fat, and in no time at all had a baby on their knees.

'Now these old men, who were brothers, lived in a beggarly cottage in the lee of a great wood that overlooked the bend of a river, whose name I've forgotten; and one night — or so he pretended — the blind poet of Otterburn, having lost his way, stumbled against its gable-wall, and heard the wicked old men singing inside. So he listened at the window, and what they were singing, over and over again, was this:

> Ha, ha, hah!
>   Hee, hee, hee!
> Open the door, it's only me!
> Ha, ha, hah!
>   Ho, ho, hoh!
> Here's a stick to lay you low!

'So the blind poet, having discovered where he was, and when he had committed to memory what the old men were singing, went home and spent the next three days thinking about the wicked brothers who daunted a whole countryside with their great cudgels; and in the following three days he made a song about them, that my mother used to sing to sailors and people of that sort. And now, if you're agreeable and ready to join in the chorus, I'll sing it to you.'

There were fifty-one verses in the song, and after every half-dozen or so Albyn would call for another round of mead, and the Oldest Druid would say to the young men beside him, his wrinkled face all creased with laughter, 'It's a naughty song! A very naughty song indeed. I can't approve of it at all, and the King wouldn't like it, I'm sure.' — But the young soldiers, stamping their feet, grew hoarse with singing, and when the last chorus had been sung the grave young man with the black brows exclaimed: 'This is as good a song as we're likely to hear in our time, and it's a shame to keep it to ourselves. I say we should go out and sing it in the streets, and let all Wigtown hear it!'

Everyone except the Oldest Druid thought this a fine suggestion, for they were in a mood to applaud any bold or lively plan. So Albyn pulled open the door, and though the snow was falling again they hurried out, with the dark young man in the lead, laughing and shouting to each other in the darkness. But the Oldest Druid, left all alone, took a horn and a little cask in which there was still a quart or so of mead, and sat himself down in the fireplace, as near as he could get to the bright red logs, for comfort and for warmth.

Albyn and the young men, marching into Wigtown, sang so loudly and their song was so inviting that quickly some three or four hundred citizens came out and joined them, men and women too, and presently they were not only singing but dancing in the town square. The snow stopped and the moon came out to light the feathered whiteness of the ground, and sturdy householders, roused from their beds, brought tubs of new ale to keep the dancers leaping and moisten the throats of the pipers and the flute-players who, drawn by the noise of singing, had come to make the dancers lift their heels another foot or so above the ground.

Soon all the town was dancing there, in the candid light of a full unsullied moon, and among the women Albyn saw Ferli, heavy with her child but eager for a spring. He took her by the hands and drew her into a reel, and Ferli stepped as high and swung as merrily as any in the square. Their reel finished, the dark young man claimed her for another, and before it was half done the snow came down again, the moon was dimmed, and while the pipers kept the shrill tune leaping above the solemn drones, the dancers all put on a cloak of whiteness an inch thick; and when the last figure was concluded the dark young man shouted for Albyn. — 'The song!' he cried. 'Let's have the song again, it's too dark for dancing.'

So Albyn, while the soft flakes fell, told again the story of the two old men with their cudgels of life and death, and the people of Wigtown listened closely and laughed loudly; and when he sang the chorus they took it up so lustily they blew the falling snow away. Then someone — it may have been the dark young man — cried out: 'Let's sing our song to Furbister! Let Furbister enjoy his Yule! Furbister should hear our song, and Bala too!'

They made a hearty but untidy procession then, and marching to the palace, like an army of snow-men, made Albyn sing his song, and all with great delight joined in the chorus:

'Ha, ha, hah!
    Hee, hee, hee!
Open the door, it's only me!
Ha, ha, hah!
    Ho, ho, hoh!
Here's a stick to lay you low!'

But though they sang it fifty-one times, after every verse, the palace remained dark and forbidding, and neither Furbister nor Bala came out to thank them for their singing and wish them well in the New Year. They grumbled a little, but the moon shone clear again, and most of them went back to bed within the next hour or so.

In Albyn's house, Liss had had her supper and gone to bed at her usual time. Undisturbed by the young men's singing in the hall, she had slept soundly for several hours, then wakened uneasily. She smelt something burning, she thought, and clutching a blanket round her, she went into the hall.

The Oldest Druid, sitting in the chimney-place, was pouring a horn of mead over the skirt of his long woollen cloak, which a spluttering log had set on fire. He was leaning over the warm grey ashes, in the thick smoke that rose from them, but unperturbed by his danger and blissfully at peace. In a cracked uncertain voice he was singing, out of season, one of the hymns for Beltane.

'It's time you were in bed,' said Liss, and helped him to his feet.

'Time was and time shall be, and sleep can't stop it,' he said; but without more protest he let her lead him to a pile of sheepskins by the wall, and lay down contentedly enough.

CHAPTER TWENTY-TWO

WHEN Albyn was summoned to appear before Furbister to answer for his ill-behaviour in provoking what was said to have been a riot, he was shocked to see that Furbister had adopted the Carrick style of audience. Evening had fallen, and torch-bearers in a double rank lighted a lane through the great hall to a dais where Furbister and Bala sat side by side on their chairs within a semi-circle of more torches. To prepare for war against Od McGammon, Furbister had already introduced a form of conscription almost as severe as Od McGammon's; but that he should copy his neighbour of Carrick in the matter of torches was, to Albyn, singularly displeasing. It was Albyn who had told him of Carrick's torch-bearers.

Furbister spoke harshly and at great length about Albyn's wild conduct, which had not only disturbed the whole town, he said, but broken his nuptial sleep. Men had been punished with death for smaller offences, he declared, and Albyn himself would have been in danger of his life had not Bala most graciously spoken on his behalf.

'I reminded him,' said Bala, smiling like the new moon tossing in a stormy sky, 'that we are much indebted to you. Had it not been for you, dear Furbister and I might never have met.'

'I could also claim,' said Albyn boldly, 'to have been of service to you in the matter of getting rid of Od McGammon when he came here.'

'Nonsense!' exclaimed Furbister. 'I got rid of him! He put his finger in my mouth, and I bit it to the bone. And then he ran away!'

'But it was Albyn's idea,' said Bala, 'that you should lie in a cradle to receive him.'

'And what good would that have done,' demanded Furbister, 'if I hadn't bitten his finger? It was biting his finger that turned the trick.'

'You were very brave, and very clever,' said Bala, and looked at Albyn with a little frown to keep him quiet.

'Well,' said Albyn, 'I'm sorry if I spoiled your sleep, but I have a cheerful nature on the whole, and it seems to me that any country is the better for a certain number of people whose disposition is lively and sanguine; and I don't think it's good policy to punish them for it. I'm a poet too, and if a poet hasn't a certain amount of exuberance, he might as well look for another trade.'

'I'm glad you brought that up,' said Furbister, 'for I've been thinking about poetry, and especially about the epic you've promised me. How are you getting on with it, by the way?'

'Very well,' said Albyn. 'Very well indeed.'

'Have you begun to compose it yet?'

'Oh no! Nor shall I for another six or seven years.'

'That's what I thought,' said Furbister, 'and in the meantime I believe we can provide you with some useful experience. — A good many of our songs about war and fighting, and so forth, seem to have been made by people who had never actually taken part in a campaign; and it's my opinion that you ought to get some practical knowledge of war before you begin your poem. So instead of condemning you to death, I've decided you shall serve in my army from tomorrow till the end of hostilities; and if you're lucky enough to survive, I'm sure you'll be grateful to me for the opportunity I'm giving you.'

'I don't take very kindly to discipline,' said Albyn. 'I'm afraid I shall never make a good soldier.'

'I don't suppose you will,' Furbister agreed. 'But even as a bad soldier you ought to learn something to your advantage.'

In the gloomiest of moods Albyn retired from the palace, and on the following morning one of Furbister's sergeants called for him and escorted him to the town barracks. A few days later he was removed to a training-ground some ten miles from Wigtown, and there, being asked which arm of the service he would prefer to join, he became a slinger: for a slinger, he thought, standing at a little distance from the main battle, might observe it clearly without becoming too intimately engaged in it. He should be able to see its pattern better than a swordsman or a spearman, whose vision would certainly be obscured by the unpleasant proximity of the enemy. A measure of detachment was often advisable in life. — 'Put me down as a slinger,' said Albyn.

Day after day he drilled in cold weather with his chance companions, and for the first week or two disliked extremely his new mode of life. But then he began to grow interested in the art of slinging pebbles at a target — and then at moving targets, and the concerted slinging of a whole troop, and the delightful craft of taking cover — and he was even aware of some little pride in his improving marksmanship, when news arrived that dispelled his small growth of comfort, and cast him into such a mingled gloom of guilt and sadness as he had never known before.

Ferli, after her dancing in the snow, had fallen ill, and presently given birth to a premature baby that died a few days later. — Now Albyn had had only the smallest desire of seeing Ferli's child: in moments of bravado he had indeed thought of it as the evidence of a poet's exuberant virility, but more sensibly and far more often he had looked forward to its birth with discomfort and foreboding. It would be a bondage and a burden on him — and he could not deny that its untimely death was a relief. But its death, he realized, was a grief, that he would never fathom, insufferably added to poor Ferli's loneliness. And for Ferli he felt a sorrow that he could not expiate even by slinging pebbles harder and more accurately than ever before.

Then he heard that Liss, all sense of grievance overwhelmed by sympathy, had taken Ferli to live with her; and Albyn's unhappiness was mixed with a small irrational annoyance, and a little discoloured by jealousy.

CHAPTER TWENTY-THREE

ONE of the troopers who accompanied Od Mc-Gammon on his ill-starred visit to Galloway had not returned with him. Being of an inflammable disposition, he had fallen in love with a Wigtown girl, and finding an opportunity to desert, had got a home with her and her parents. Neither she nor they had a very good name in the town, but for a couple of months the deserter lived easily enough with them, and loudly declared that Galloway suited him forty times better than ever Carrick had. Then, however, he began to quarrel with the girl, for reasons that most men would have found sufficient, and a little while after Yule there was a family brawl in which she and her mother and her father all turned against him, and threw him out.

Bruised and bleeding, and suddenly full of hatred for the country whose people had betrayed him, the deserter decided to return to Carrick and tell Od McGammon all he had learnt of Furbister's preparation for war. There had been little snow as yet, and the hill-roads were still open. He knew, moreover, the disposition of the light forces that watched the frontier, for one of the men on duty there — but coming back on leave to Wigtown — had been his girl's latest lover; and the deserter had listened sullenly to his tales of their lonely service.

He found little difficulty, then, and less danger, in the first part of his journey; but no sooner had he crossed the border than snow fell heavily, and losing his way in the storm he would have died of cold had he not stumbled by chance against the wall of a lonely cottage. When he reached Ayr he had a good story to tell of the hardships he had endured, and frost-bitten ears and toes to show in proof of them. His story was listened to, and when he told Od McGammon that Furbister, whom he had often seen, was in truth no bigger than the Caretaker himself, Od McGammon's elation was so great that he gave the deserter a free pardon. Then he sent out his officers to warn the whole country that Galloway was preparing war, and summon every man to arms against the tyrant Furbister.

This news of a foreign enemy came just in time to prevent the outbreak of a great rebellion against Od McGammon. Since Albyn's tale of the love that life needed to make it whole — which he still believed to be a deliberate and bitter mockery of him — Od McGammon had stiffened the severity of his rule, to prove his own system right; and his unhappy people, driven to desperation, were plotting immediate revolt. But when they heard of Furbister's intention, they were perplexed and their purpose weakened. Then Od McGammon spread stories of the barbaric and un-scrupulous habits of the men of Galloway, and the Carrick people, being frightened beyond measure by his description of their savage opponents, came to the conclusion that they must stand loyally by the Care-taker and help him to defend their wives and children against the unspeakable humiliation and appalling torments which would otherwise be their lot. So the whole of Carrick became an armed camp, and its people were united as never before in their heroic determination to resist the onslaught of Furbister and his abominable regiments. Od McGammon, however, was planning to anticipate Furbister's assault, and launch the first attack himself.

About a month after the Carrick deserter's return, one of the Druids whom King Glam had been forced to leave behind him, escaped and took refuge with a woman who still believed in the old religion despite the suppression of its priesthood. She found others to befriend him, and after a week or so during which he lived in considerable danger, he succeeded in crossing the frontier. He told Furbister of Od McGammon's huge and desperate preparation for war, and a few days later all Galloway was in a new ferment of fear and hatred.

In both countries stories began to circulate of strange signs and portents. — A lamb had been born with five legs, a duckling with two heads had been hatched. In Tarbolton there had been a fall of hailstones as big as a man's fist, in Ecclefechan a shower of blood. An old man had prophesied the end of the world, a young woman had been got with child by a ghost. Trees fell flat on windless nights, hillsides gaped open and belated travellers disappeared. Shooting-stars crisscrossed the sky, the Northern Lights shone red as gore, and children everywhere repeated a drunkard's story of two moons that bounced upon a roaring cloud until they burst.

It was in a mood, then, of wild belief, extravagant fear, and superstitious hatred that the two armies set out on the first Monday in April, each followed by a vast unruly crowd of old men, women, and children. For Furbister and Od McGammon, urging all speed on their officers and watching the weather for the first assured promise of spring, had both been equally energetic and alert; and chosen the same day on which to march.

CHAPTER TWENTY-FOUR

IN the wilderness of hills that rose between the lowlands of Galloway and the fields of Carrick, there was a valley that the Galloway people called the Blind Glen, and in Carrick was known as the Glen of the Cliff. At its upper end — the closed or blind end — a stream ran down in ragged waterfalls from rough, impassable, broken ground above, and in early spring, after the snows had melted, the floor of the valley was soft and treacherous. In its lower parts there were marshes in which the earth melted and would suck a man down, and the stream divided and ran in narrow, half-hidden rivulets.

The Cliff, that gave it its other name, was an outcrop of rock on the Galloway side, a small grey platform, perhaps twenty yards long, just under the top of the slope. As a cliff it was unremarkable, for the face of it was only six or eight feet high; but it afforded a commanding view of the glen.

Now the main forces of Furbister and Od McGammon were fast approaching in one of the broad passes through the hills when their scouts became aware of each other; and Furbister and Od McGammon, at the same moment, made the same tactical decision. — It would be an admirable move, they decided, to take up a defensive position on the rim of the Blind Glen, and force the enemy to advance over soft and swampy ground, and then attack uphill. So each made a turning movement, one to the right and the other to the left, and presently their armies faced each other across the steep green valley, and began shouting all the insults they could think of. Well established on hard high ground, they were both prepared to meet the attack. But after they had stood there for about an hour it became evident that neither side was eager to attack.

Both armies, painted for battle, looked extremely fierce and warlike, and in their chequered plaids — yellows and many shades of green on the one side, russet and red and brown and different blues on the other — they made a gallant and splendid spectacle. But neither side would move from its good position, and Furbister and Od McGammon grew perplexed and short of temper.

The women and children and the old men who had followed the armies now pressed close behind them, taunting their soldiers and loudly asking what they were frightened of. The soldiers had brought this on themselves; for they had been boasting for many weeks of what they would do to the enemy, and their women-folk had had a very difficult and miserable life with them. On the one hand the women had been extremely frightened by all the stories of the opposing side's atrocious habits; and on the other hand they had been exasperated beyond endurance by their own men's unceasing talk of the war, and how quickly they would win it. So now they were in a hurry to get the battle over, and be done with their fears and boredom too; and they taunted their soldiers with increasing bitterness.

The soldiers on both sides grew restless and ill at ease. As well as the clatter of the women's tongues, the air was noisy with a great crying of birds. Vast flocks of crows and kites, of ravens and buzzards and eagles too, were gathering above the valley, attracted by the living smell of humanity and excited by their greedy expectation of its death. Their hoarse voices fretted the soldiers' nerves, their wings darkened the sky, as if the sun was shrinking and going out. — Someone on the Carrick side said an old woman had told him the sun would never rise again if Carrick was defeated; and quickly the rumour spread. Among the Galloway men, about the same time, a story was whispered that the seasons had gone awry, because of a curse upon the land, and henceforward their summer would be darker than winter. The air grew colder, so it seemed, and men looked upward with foreboding eyes at the wings that filled the sky like angry clouds.

Now Furbister, standing on the platform of the Cliff, with Bala beside him, in the middle of the valley, decided to send out his light forces, his slingers, to harass and sting the enemy, and so provoke them, if they could, to an assault. — The rest of the army cheered; and the slingers, Albyn among them, went down into the valley in a long thin line, each man choosing his way. Liss, who stood with Ferli and her father a little apart from the other followers, saw Albyn's red head moving against the green, and bit her lip and clutched a hand to her breast.

Od McGammon had light forces too. On either wing of his army stood a company of archers, who, he had intended, would keep on the fringes of the fight and choose their targets with care. For they were not very good archers, their bows being short and incapable of shooting far. But now, a little alarmed by the advance of Furbister's slingers, who were said to be redoubtable, he decided to use his archers as a screen in front of his main forces; and they also were ordered into the valley.

The archers and the slingers, who all fancied themselves as marksmen and despised the brutalities of hand-to-hand conflict, settled down to an exchange of shots; and as most of them chose positions at the extreme limit of their range, their shooting was pretty but ineffectual.

The followers, the women and children and old men, had watched their advance with excitement and applause; but they were quickly displeased by such cautious behaviour, and took to jeering and mocking more loudly than before. The carrion birds, moreover, their flocks growing ever more numerous, were now flying lower, hungry for the first death; and the chorus of their rough voices rose to a frenzied scream that tormented the minds of the waiting soldiers.

It was Bala who first lost patience and began the general movement. Bala had never shown any appreciation of tactics, or the value of high ground; and now, incensed by the slingers' caution and catching from the soldiers on either side the infection of their deep unease, she leapt from the Cliff and went striding with great paces down into the glen towards the nearest of Od McGammon's archers. She carried a heavy club, the trunk of a young tree, and waved it furiously.

Furbister shouted to her in vain, and from the opposing army came a bellow of mingled fear and hatred. — Bala, indifferent to arrows ill aimed by frightened men, clouted the foremost archer, and immediately a score of carrion birds came swooping down upon him. She ran to catch another, who had taken to his heels, and a moment later was caught in soft ground and sank above her knees. She struggled to get clear, and cried for help.

Now Furbister, with a great shout of anguish, jumped from the Cliff and ran to her rescue, lumbering but fast. Released by his example from the intolerable strain of waiting — waiting while their women mocked, and the carrion birds screamed above — his army followed, pouring like a green wave into the valley. But Bala, stuck fast in the mud, was nearer to the Carrick side, and Od McGammon had seen his chance to capture her. Leading two hundred men — 'Let the rest stand fast!' he shouted — he hurried down to seize her, but forty yards from the struggling giantess felt the ground yielding, and grew cautious. His men, more lightly built, came nearer but dared not lay hands on Bala.

Mindless of the bog, Furbister went in knee-deep, reached out his hands to Bala, and heaved with all his strength to pull her free. He sank deeper with the effort, but hauled her out and floundered on to firmer ground himself. He stood breathing deeply, mud to the mid-thigh, but Bala was besmeared all over. Then he saw that Od McGammon, a crowd of soldiers with him, had found a passage through the mire and was closing for the fight. He stooped for the club he had thrown down — no smith could forge a sword for giants — and the wooden din, when club met giant's club, resounded in the valley like ice-floes in a river cracking and grinding in a thaw.

The battle now was general, for Od McGammon's army, despite his last order, had followed the first two hundred into the glen, and both forces were locked in conflict and fettered deep in mud. Though not a marsh, like its lower part, the valley at this time of year was water-logged, and here and there were patches of yielding bog. There was no order in the battle, but swordsmen and spearmen fought side by side, with slingers in their midst; and having once advanced to the encounter they could hardly retreat. Trampled into a morass, the floor of the valley grew softer and more yielding, the mud caught at men's heels, they stumbled and struck wildly at the nearest foe. They were maddened by the clinging mud and driven to a senseless fury by the savage screaming of the birds, that covered with their beating wings each man who fell, and tore his flesh while it was still warm with life. From far and wide ravens and carrion-crows, kites and buzzards and ernes and golden eagles came fleet-winged to the red havoc in the valley; and now on either rim, on their knees, the women and children were sobbing, and praying, and screaming like the kites.

Furbister, yielding ground to Od McGammon but giving blow for blow, had fought his way back to a slope of turf below the Cliff. Unnerved by her struggle in the bog, and fear of drowning in it, Bala gave him no help but kept close behind him. On either side of them men fought with the utmost fury, as though incapable of any thought of yielding; and the two giants, so long afraid of each other, revealed in the violence of their strokes and their hideous grimaces the rage that for years had smouldered in their minds. Their painted faces were great masks of hatred, and their huge bodies, from which their breath escaped in angry squalls, were labouring like winter seas with murderous effort. In all the valley there was only one

man who had kept his senses and was untouched by the
infection of wrath; and that was Albyn. When the
hurly-burly had closed upon him, and his sling was no
longer of use, Albyn had picked up a spear that a dead
man no longer wanted, and by prudent management
of it had succeeded in keeping himself somewhat aloof
from the tussle. Now, like Bala, he was sheltering
behind Furbister's strenuous back.

Slowly the sun moved down the sky, as though
retreating from the howling fury of the battle, and on
the slope of turf below the Cliff the giants, both
bruised and bleeding, broke their clubs in a last
furious blow that Furbister dealt and Od McGammon
warded. Then, after pausing a minute to breathe again—
and their breathing sounded like a storm in a forest —
they grappled and fumbled for each other's throats.
Now Bala, her courage regained and seeing that Furbister was in difficulties, let out a howl of consternation
and with her great fists beat like a shoeing-smith on
Od McGammon's back. This brought three Carrick
spearmen to the Caretaker's aid, and Bala howled again
to feel sharp iron in her calf. Well aware that he was
being foolish, but yielding to a generous impulse,
Albyn attacked the Carrick men, and a moment later
was trapped, as if in a coppice of madly dancing trees,
among the huge and stiffly moving legs of the wrestling
giants.

Between the foot of the Cliff and the slope of grass
a crack appeared, that broadened into a little gulf, as
the earth gave way under their convulsive weight.
They staggered sideways, and Bala lost her balance.
She fell, and her knee pinned Albyn to the ground.
She tried to rise, but Furbister and Od McGammon

came down upon her in a dog-fall, and broke her neck. In her last convulsive movement she dug a living grave for Albyn, and above it the giants of Galloway and Carrick thrashed to and fro in a grip that neither would relax, and died in each other's wrathful arms.

In all the valley there was now no sign of life but the frenzy of the carrion birds. Now it was their turn to fight, and the floor of the valley, where the dead lay sprawling under their beaks and wings, seemed to be covered with a ragged carpet that flapped and fluttered in a gusty wind. But the April sun shone brightly above the western hills, the sky was unclouded and empty now.

The old men and women and children, of Galloway and Carrick too, had fled the scene. Desolate and overwhelmed with grief, they had been stricken by a fear, spreading as if a breeze had carried it, that the birds were the spirits of evil, more rapacious of men's souls than of their bodies. In panic fear they fled to their empty villages and silent homes, and the Blind Glen was left in possession of crows and kites, of ravens, and the great eagles of the mountains and the sea.

CHAPTER TWENTY-FIVE

WHEN Liss and her father, and Ferli with them, returned to the valley two days later, they saw it as if it were the floor of a sea from which the waters had receded to show the wreckage of two great fleets that once had sailed upon it. The ribs and strong timbers of the sunken ships, washed white, shone bare and pale in a mild air beneath a tempered sun. The valley was littered with bones, well made and strongly fashioned. The multitude of carrion birds had picked them clean, and they lay on the soft and treacherous ground as if they were the ruins of humankind. But the birds, full-fed and somnolent, had gathered on the slopes of the valley — blanched with their droppings — and roosted there, grunting and croaking when they woke. On the flatter parts, among the bones, the lesser birds of the air had now come for the remnants of the feast. There were finches and robins, terns from the sea-shore, starlings glittering in the sun and mottled thrushes, and sparrows and woodpeckers. There was a twittering of many small voices in the valley, there were runlets and the rippling of song.

Only Liss and Ferli and King Glam had dared return. All the others, the widows and bereaved mothers and fatherless children of Galloway and Carrick, were mourning their dead but so frightened of the evil spirits in the valley that they would not come to give them burial. — Liss, like the rest of them, had fled in horror and lain stricken with grief. She had stood, in a little crowd of women, on the platform of the Cliff and seen the wrestling of the giants and Albyn's disappearance under their tumbling weight. She had run in fear, when the carrion flocks came down and panic spread; but her remembrance of panic had gone like the half-memory of a nightmare, and hope came up again as if it were a swimmer's head in a desolate sea. — She had not seen Albyn dead. There was no warrant or certainty of his death.

The old King, her father, said his people had their rights in death, as they had had in life; and he must see to their proper disposal. Ferli, who had had a spring-time love for Albyn, had now a riper love, like harvest and its gain, for Liss. She would go with them, she said, if they wanted her.

They stood on the platform of the Cliff and looked down at the valley and the pale bones scattered on its green. Below them lay the enormous brittle skeletons of the giants, their ribs already crumbling, their long shanks splintered, and white flakes peeling from their haunches as though from huge clay basins. Their bones, it seemed, could not endure exposure to the air, but pores and fissures opened, they cracked in the sun and powder sifted from a broken edge. The wind blew stronger, and the knuckle-bones of a great hand were blown away like dust. — On the trampled ground, pot-holed and scarred by the violence of their death-struggle, there lay a leather-sling that might have been Albyn's; but Albyn's body had disappeared, and Liss, feeling her mouth as dry as the dust that had been a giant, said in a breaking voice, 'He is not dead, I do not believe he is dead. He will come back.'

They climbed down from the Cliff and stood among

the powdering bones. Old Glam put his hand on a skull as big as a washing tub, and it crumbled at his touch. He blew upon his fingers and said, 'There are many of my people here. We must give them burial.'

'Can we tell our own from those who were strangers?' asked Liss.

'They fought together, they can lie together,' said Glam. 'There is no difference now.'

They went down into the valley and began to gather the bones together, and build them into cairns. Tattered clothing lay about, there were plaids of many colours, but which haunches had worn the green and which the blue it was often impossible to say. The carrion birds had been strong and savage, and sometimes a leg-bone lay far from the case of ribs it had carried.

All day Liss and her father and Ferli laboured, and the small birds, pecking here and there, whistled and sang. At night they lay down on the Cliff on a heap of plaids that Ferli had collected. Ferli looked after them, and found food for them that the soldiers had brought, but had no time to eat. Old Glam slept soundly, but Liss lay weeping, and Ferli tried to comfort her.

They laboured another day, gathering the bones and piling them together. Many of the skeletons, and the plaids they had worn, lay in the narrow channels of the stream, damming the water; and sometimes, when the water was released, it fetched away a part of the bank. The valley was very wet, but old Glam and the two women worked steadily, and when darkness fell they had built a line of cairns that glimmered palely in the dusk. They lay down again on the Cliff, over the cracked turf where Albyn had disappeared, and hidden by the darkness Liss was weeping. Ferli lay awake for a long time, but fell asleep at last and slept until the first light of dawn was in the sky. Then she woke to hear the rumbling noise of earth falling, and a cry from Liss.

Liss, on her knees, was looking down at the slope of grass where the giants had wrestled. A crack had opened, while they fought, between the top of the slope and the foot of the Cliff; but now the earth had fallen away altogether, and uncovered a seated figure whose face was pale and whose hair caught enough light from the breaking sky to show a reddish hue.

He stretched his arms and put his head back, yawning. A huge toad jumped off his knee, and disappeared in a crevice in the earth. He turned, and saw Liss and Ferli on the Cliff.

'You've come for me too soon,' said Albyn. 'I've been making a poem, and it's not finished yet.'

CHAPTER TWENTY-SIX

'YOU are cold as the earth itself,' said Liss. 'You smell of the earth.'

They had helped him up the Cliff and wrapped him in the torn plaids of the dead. He sat on the rock, and Liss and Ferli, crouched on either side of him, rubbed his hands. The old King, roused from sleep, lay watching them but did not speak.

Albyn too was silent for a little while. Then, speaking softly as if to himself — his head hanging, his chin on his breast — he said, 'The giants are no more. They crushed me in their fall, but they lay where they fell and the wind blew their bones away. Then I stood up again.'

'Thank Liss for that!' cried Ferli. 'She wept all night for you, this night and last night, and her tears melted the earth!'

'Nonsense,' said old Glam. 'You're talking nonsense, girl. All the streams were choked for several days, but now that we've cleared them the water's running fast, and the banks are giving way. That's all there is to it.'

Albyn seemed not to have heard them, and slowly and quietly as before went on speaking. 'I have made in my mind,' he said, 'three lines of a poem, but I could not make the last one. It is a poem to make men live, as the best poems do; but I cannot finish it. Could I make it whole it would give life again to those who died before their time, fighting for the giants.'

'That is in no man's power,' said the old King.

'There are words in our speech,' said Albyn, 'that are like the Standing Stones an earlier people set up, here and there, in our fields. They are very old, and like the Standing Stones they cast shadows, and in their shadows a man may dream. Now there are dreams that live longer than their dreamers, and words that make deeds of long ago done yet again tomorrow. Set words in their proper order — each throwing a shadow that holds a dream — and you may fashion verses that will outlive all giants and tyrannies, and set men unborn to singing, to worship, or to war. There is life beyond the life of a man in words, and a spell to make men live or die. — But my spell's unfinished, I cannot make it whole!'

'Tell me what you have made,' said Liss.

'A thing half-made is made for mockery,' said Albyn, 'and a fragment should not be spoken.'

'Whisper it, then,' said Liss, and led him to the far end of the Cliff. She felt his lips cold against her ear, and listened and said, 'I can tell you the last line now — but you would never have learnt it for yourself though you had lived a twelvemonth under the ground, with the toad on your knee and the earth betraying to you all the secrets of earth! It's too simple for you to think of, and too hard for you to understand; for you never loved the men whom now you want to save. I've told you before, and I tell you again that though you take pleasure in people, you don't love people for themselves. And without love you can't do so great a thing as make dead bones live.'

'Tell me the last line,' he said, and shivered with the warmth of her mouth at his cheek. But he shook his head, and answered, 'No, I can't understand.'

'Fool that you are!' she cried. 'There's Ferli and my father there, without a quarter of your wit, and both of them know what I mean! — Come, listen, and you'll hear. And it may be our love will give you warmth again, for you're cold through and through, like the earth you come from.'

She led him back and made Ferli and the old King get up, and take each other's hands. They stood in a circle, Albyn between Liss and Ferli, the old King opposite, and Liss declared: 'Let him listen to his own spell, that he could not finish and that I have finished for him. And though it does no other good, it may give me a warmer husband to take home with me.'

Then, in a clear high voice, Liss declaimed the three lines that Albyn had made, and the fourth that she had added; and their hands clung together as though they would never loose their grip, and Albyn cried out in pain as their warmth went through him like the blood coming back after frostbite. Then Ferli let go his hand, and the old King's hand, and pointed to the valley, grey in the half-light before dawn. 'Look,' she whispered. 'Look!'

The white cairns were moving, as though the earth heaved under them, and as they fell apart the bones clattered in the stillness of the valley. From the nearest cairn a skull rolled to the grass, and skeleton fingers reached for it and set it like a crown in its proper place. Out of the narrow bed of a stream a leg-bone rose, and tottered off in search of its fellow shank. The little bones of a severed foot, and finger-bones lopped off by a rusting sword, rattled together like dice in a cup; and lost arms beckoned to branchless ribs. They moved slowly at first, in a blind and stumbling way, but gradually their movement quickened, and became impatient. Shin-bones clattered loudly, hurrying to find their own, and rattled over recumbent ribs. Skulls knocked with a hollow note, rolling on the green, and thigh-bones like great clubs beat knuckle-bones aside. A pair of shoulder-blades clapped together, a collar-bone beat a tattoo on the hollow of a haunch. — But now more and more skeletons stood erect, moving a little jerkily, but whole and complete; and as the sun came up to the horizon the last of the little bones found their proper place, and the dead soldiers, though lifeless still, were on their feet again.

The eastern sky grew red, the white skeletons were flushed with a rosy hue, and a blur of light covered their bones. The sun came up, bright gold, and the watchers were dazzled by its level rays. They rubbed their eyes, and looked again, and saw that the valley was full of living men.

The soldiers drew their first breath, and shouted for joy. They danced and leapt, and felt their strength again. Friend or foe, they clasped each other to their naked breasts, and cried, and wiped away their tears with impatient hands, and laughed, and talked in wild half-words and broken sentences. They hurried hither and thither, looking for comrades, and then on the Cliff saw Liss and Albyn, Ferli and old King Glam.

They ran towards them, and gathered below the Cliff, and shouted their praise. They saw that Albyn had felt the coldness of the earth, and come back to life again; they thought it was he alone who had found words to lift the burden of their death, for Liss, behind him, stood hand in hand with Ferli, claiming no credit. Their shouting rose high and shrill over a deeper burden, and swelled and sank again in a natural rhythm; and then they fell silent, and stood expectantly. — A bearded man of Carrick stood forward and spoke, and when he had done, a black-browed, thin-faced youth of Galloway took up his theme and expounded it with a readier tongue. They both demanded that Albyn, who had given them life, should now rule them, the men of both nations together, with absolute power over all, and tell them from day to day how to live.

Liss grew anxious, her face looked thin and wary, and the King muttered, 'Fools! Will they never learn?' — But a minute later old Glam was nodding his head contentedly, and Liss, like a young mother whose child was behaving well, wore a look of proud delight.

Albyn, flushed with life again, had stepped forward and shouted in a passion, 'No, no, no! Haven't you had enough of the ills that come upon you when you submit to a giant's rule? And what should I be, if I governed you, but a little man puffed up with power to play a giant's part? Can't you see that no man, whatever his goodwill, has the knowledge or the wisdom to say to his fellow-men, "Do this, and do that!"? — Good men, men of experience working together, can say, "*Don't* do this, *don't* do that. You mustn't kill, you mustn't rob, nor malign your neighbours, nor rape their daughters, nor discredit God who made you." But only bad men, or unhappy and therefore untrustworthy men, or men with no experience of living, will try to tell their fellow-men how they must spend their lives. — O God, what presumption it were to do so! What man alive has ruled his own life to the satisfaction of his conscience? And how then should any man, having failed in that little trial, have the arrogance to lay down rules for a multitude? No, no, my friends — my fellow-soldiers and my enemies, between whom I can find no scrap of difference now that your mad leaders have killed each other. No, no! We're mortal men, and though our eyes are good enough to see a manifest evil, and we've minds that tell us to avoid or punish it, we cannot yet discern the immanent general good; and we've no right to make positive laws that shall harness a whole nation to our own weak fancy of its nature. — Go home, I say, and learn to rule yourselves. You won't succeed, but your faults will be small compared with a giant's faults and the follies of a giant's government. Try to rule yourselves, and when you look at your neighbours remember that what gave you life again was not law but love! Be positive in love, keep law for saying no! — And now go home, live your own lives as best you can, and let me live mine!'

CHAPTER TWENTY-SEVEN

THE oldest inhabitant, who was a hundred and five, had never known such weather. Day after day broke fine and windless, what rain was necessary for the fields fell only at night, and the heat of midday was always mitigated in the afternoon by a gentle but sufficient breeze from the south or west. For six months after the battle in the Blind Glen there was neither gale nor drenching rain, nor fog nor drought in Galloway; and the behaviour of the people was equally remarkable.

From the Rhinns to the valley of the Esk the clans and little kingdoms that Furbister swept away had been re-established, and there was no dispute between them. Nor, within the clans and their villages, had there been any overt contention between neighbours. Even in the family circle quarrelling almost ceased; and throughout the country crime vanished completely. Wonderment and awe still lay upon the land, and the men who had been killed in battle, and come to life again, spoke more quietly than had been their custom; while their women-folk wore a new aspect of complacency.

It was Ferli who was responsible for the look of satisfaction, smooth as cream, that the women wore. Ferli told everyone, with unwearying repetition, that really it was Liss who had worked the miracle. Liss's tears, she said, had melted the earth and let Albyn out of his living tomb, and Liss had contributed the most important line to the spell that he had in part devised. It was woman's gift of love, and her knowledge of love's supremacy, declared Ferli, that had given them back their husbands and their lovers, their brothers and sons. No one disputed Albyn's cleverness, but without Liss's better part, his cleverness had been of no avail. It was woman, said Ferli, who had re-made their world — she was the creative power — and by her example it should be ruled.

There was a woman in Borgue, well known as the angriest shrew and loudest termagant in all Galloway, who listened with incredulity and dismay to the new doctrine that love must rule, and women were its ministers of state. She thought for a day or two, and then went down to the sea and drowned herself. — But others of the same sort perceived their advantage under the new order, and by subduing their temper made their husbands believe that the miracle in the valley was spreading farther. Everywhere there reigned a sort of benign superstition, and the land prospered as never before.

To begin with, the Oldest Druid had been worried by a secret fear that Albyn and Liss, on the strength of their remarkable achievement, would set themselves up as the priests of a new spiritual order; and he had advised parochial Druids, throughout the country, to say as little as possible of the revival of the bones, and on no account to preach about it. But when he found that neither Liss nor Albyn was emulous of power, or greedy for authority, he changed his tune and proclaimed the miracle to be an avowal of the true essence of the universe, and Galloway the chosen land of revelation.

Love, he said in a notable sermon that was widely discussed, was at once the prime cause of life and the necessary condition of its perfection. Let them not underestimate the woman's share in the miracle, for a woman moved by love might be a symbol as well as an agent. — Whether the Creator was Male or Female no mortal could be sure; and the Druids had always kept an open mind about it. When one considered how little was the part that reason played in life, one could not exclude the possibility that the Great Author of life was Female; and if now there should be some increasing tendency to accept that view — now that they had seen in its potency the creative will of a woman's love — why, he the High Priest of all the Druids would never invoke the sanctions of the Church against it, but humble in his own uncertainty, would multiply his faith in the Causative Benignity by the measure of his own ignorance. That their dear princess, the Princess Liss, was a saint, he had little doubt; and Albyn her husband was one of the most promising young poets in the south-west of Scotland ...

Albyn was less pleased by this sermon than the majority of those who heard of it; many of whom were women. He thought he deserved more credit than he had had, but no one else seemed to be upset by the injustice he had suffered; and to all the stories that Ferli had spread, the sermon now gave the full authority of the Church. Love ruled the land and women were its ministers, conscious of their power; while the men who had tasted death were in no mood to gainsay that which had rescued them from it.

And the land prospered. Men worked upon their fields as though in gratitude, and no one asked for help in vain. No one mis-spent his thoughts on hatred, or wasted another's work in envy. No one made difficulties, raised obstacles, or quarrelled to preserve his pride; but all laboured in contentment with their life, and carried water, cut firewood, whenever their wives desired it. Their wives, relieved of lesser burdens, released their benevolence in richer broth, great steaming pies, and curds and cream; and everyone grew a little fatter.

Albyn himself was infected by the prevailing kindliness, and talked to old Glam about his head shepherd's rheumatism; or listened patiently to Liss's pensioners while they told him of their early life and many ailments. He was truly gratified when Liss gave birth to a son, and only a little disappointed when she decided to call the boy, not after him, but after her father. Liss wore always a look of beatitude now, that sometimes Albyn found slightly oppressive after he had been sitting with her for an hour or two. She was like the summer weather. She was flawless, and plumper than she had been.

Autumn came, red and gold upon the leaf, clear blue across the sea to white clouds on the horizon; and Albyn took to walking far into the hills and far along the shore. He would leave his house, slightly uncomfortable about Liss's persistent happiness; and an hour later would deplore his foolish doubts. — She was right, and the whole state of Galloway proclaimed how right she was. She was lovely, moreover, far beyond the common rate of loveliness, and all her beauty was his for his enjoyment. He had no cause for unease, no cause for anything but content and gratefulness; unless he supposed beatitude to be improper for humanity.

Sometimes he met other men, walking like himself alone, and like himself perplexed. They would stop and talk together, and speak of their good fortune, the growth of the soil, and people's well-being. And then they would fall silent, and be glad when one or the other found an excuse for going on his way. — A little drunk one night, Albyn talked with Ferli, and reminded her of their journey together to the western shore. Liss was intent upon her youngest child, and Ferli, like Liss, now wore an air of constant felicity; but with a difference. Liss had all she wanted, but Ferli's happiness looked often like a temptation to come and add to it. — The autumn, said Albyn, was as good a season for walking as the spring. Would she come with him to look at the sea breaking on the Mull of Galloway, he asked?

He had not known she had such a command of words. He listened to her reproof, to her denunciation of his proposal, with gloom and respect: with gloom for the unequivocal refusal, with respect for the eloquence with which she phrased it. — He sat all night in the hall, and slept in his chair. In the morning, alone, he broke his fast on a pint of ale, a bannock of beremeal, and half a pound of bacon; and set off for the head of the bay. He had it in his mind to walk eastward for a few days, and see the country; but an hour or so after noon he met a stranger riding to the west.

The stranger was a good-looking, burly man, about forty years old, with curling hair a little grey, and a brown face seamed with an old white scar across his right cheek. A newer scar, still red and ruffled, ran up his left forearm. His eyes were blue, his nose short and straight, his chin square, and he had a lively mouth. His pony was taller by a hand than the Galloway ponies, but loose in its gait and heavy in the head from weariness.

Albyn greeted him, and the stranger said, 'My name is Ban, and I've come from York, in England. We've heard of a man called Albyn, who can raise armies from the dead; and he's the man I want to meet. Can you tell me where to find him?'

'Very easily; but what's your business with him?'

'That will keep till I see him.'

'I am Albyn.'

'You are? Then it's the very touch of fortune that's brought us together! — The matter is, that we've been fighting against the Romans, my people and I, and we need help. — But have you time to talk now, or must I wait till your work's done?'

'You would have to wait too long,' said Albyn, 'for I haven't begun it yet. So let us talk now.'

CHAPTER TWENTY-EIGHT

'THERE'S a story we've been hearing in Yorkshire,' said Ban, 'that after a battle between two of your nations here in Scotland, you made a spell that lifted the dead. It was called the Battle of the Blind Glen, according to the story, and every man fought to the death. But a week later you brought their bones to life again, and half of them went home into the north, and half came home into the south. — Now is that true?'

'That's what happened,' said Albyn. 'But it's not the whole story.'

'Never mind about details,' said Ban, 'so long as I've got the gist of it right. What's worrying us at the moment, you see, is that we've lost too many men in the last few years; but England's not conquered yet, and if we could recover our casualties, we'd show the Romans what they're up against.'

'How long have you been fighting them?'

'I myself, do you mean? — Twenty years, or more. And in that time I've seen more battles lost than won. We've had the worse of it, so far. But we're learning, at last, and they're bound to get weaker as they come farther from their base, and their lines of communication get longer and longer. We've still a good chance of turning the tide if we can keep going for another few years; and in any case I'll never give in, because I don't like them and I don't like their ways.'

'Is their discipline as strict as it's said to be?'

'On the line of march it is, and in camp it is. But

when they're on the loose they're just a lot of savages; which is what you'd expect. Their legions are recruited in Spain, and Gaul, and Germany, and the Levant: you can't call them civilized. I fought in the Icenian campaign — I'm a Norwich man, though I haven't seen it for a good many years — and sometimes, from the way they behaved, one hardly thought they were human beings. And on the line of march they don't look human either. They're too regular. I don't like straight lines, and I hate square things. But they build their roads straight, without a thought of what the country's like, and they build their camps in squares. That's their officers' fault, of course: they're less human than the men. I was a prisoner for nearly a year, and I know them. They've got no sense of beauty. They think everything ought to have right angles.'

'I don't like squares either,' said Albyn.

'They build pavements with little stones, and make patterns in them. But they're not beautiful. There's no fantasy in them. Their legions are well trained, I grant you that, but they're not the sort of people you could ever live with. Not if you've been brought up as we have, to live freely.'

'Can you hold out against them at York, do you think?'

'Well, that's where you come in: at least, I hope so. We're forming another army there, but we haven't got the numbers we need, and I don't see how we're ever going to get them — unless you can help us.'

'In what way?'

'The battle that decided the Icenian campaign was fought near Fenny Stratford, on Watling Street. It was all in the balance till then. We'd broken their Ninth Legion up by Lincoln, and we'd a hope of getting rid of them once and for all. But then they brought an army down from Wales, and we had the worst day of the war. We lost thousands on Watling Street; and they're still there. Now if you and I could get through the Roman lines — it wouldn't be difficult, for I know the whole country — and you said your spell over the dead at Fenny Stratford, we'd have an army that could take the Romans in the rear while our people at York made a pretence of starting a new offensive from north of the Humber.'

'Were many Romans killed at Fenny Stratford?'

'They must have lost almost as heavily as we did, and our losses — well, they crippled us.'

'Then if my spell worked again — and I'm by no means sure it would, because I wasn't alone in the Blind Glen — but if it did, it would bring all the Romans to life as well as the English.'

'Good God!' said Ban, shocked and dismayed.

'I thought you might be disappointed.'

'Do you mean to tell me that this spell of yours makes no distinction between one side and the other?'

'None.'

'Then it's no good at all! It's worse than that, it's extremely dangerous.'

'There are three strands in it,' said Albyn. 'There's knowledge of words, there's knowledge of men, and there's love. And love is usually unpredictable, isn't it?'

Ban looked at him curiously, and said, 'There was a part of the story, as it came to us in Yorkshire, that none of us properly understood. After the battle, so we were told, your people and the Carrick men weren't allowed to choose new leaders, but went home to be ruled — I know it sounds odd, but this is how we heard it — by love.'

'That's what it amounted to.'

'And does it work?'

'It does.'

Ban rose and whistled a melancholy tune that sounded like a funeral march; and swung the short axe he carried hanging from his wrist by a leather thong. He threw it high into the air, turning above him, and caught it by the haft as it came somersaulting down. 'It wouldn't work against the Romans,' he said. 'We'll have to depend on the old weapons still.'

'Come and talk to my wife,' said Albyn. 'I married the King's daughter, and she's at the back of it all. Our new way of life, I mean. She's quite confident, and far more convincing about it than I am.'

Ban took his tired pony by the bridle, and walked beside Albyn. 'I don't distrust a thing just because it's new,' he said. 'You mustn't think that. I've seen a lot of novelty in my time: new ideas, new instruments, new ways of training a hawk. My father invented a wolf-trap that was extraordinarily successful. — Are you much troubled with wolves here?'

'No, not here. But they're a nuisance farther north.'

'Yes, I suppose so. We don't see them in open country now, but the forest's full of them.'

A little while later he said: 'Do you think you could make another spell: a more discriminating one?'

'I'm afraid not,' said Albyn, and described the exceptional circumstances of his composition in the Blind Glen.

Ban listened gravely, and gravely apologized for the folly of his suggestion. 'I hadn't realized what you'd gone through,' he said, 'nor what your wife had done either. I'm looking forward to meeting her.'

His admiration, when he met Liss, was immediately visible; and with apparent simplicity he paid her a compliment that brought to her face a younger expression than she had lately worn. Their visitor's manner soon grew less abrupt, his haste and taut impatience were relaxed; and with the old King — who spent more and more time in his daughter's house — he was quickly at his ease.

They sat down to supper, and were two hours at table. Ban spoke at length about the Icenian war, but modestly and showing little of what he felt about his people's suffering and their defeat. The old King plied him with questions, and so did some of the young men, Albyn's friends, who sat with them; but Liss paid little and then less attention, and Ferli, at the lower end of the table, copied her expression and took pains to disregard their talk. — Ban saw he was not pleasing them, and said to Liss, 'Can you teach us a better way of dealing with these square-faced Romans? We've done what we could, and it hasn't been enough; but those of us who are still living are able to learn. Can we rule ourselves as you do, and re-arm with love?'

'But love doesn't go in armour,' said Liss. 'Love disarms.'

'Will it disarm the Romans?'

Liss looked troubled and said, 'I do not speak their language — '

'No, no!' cried Ban. 'And never learn it! I'd no thought of asking you to go as our advocate. We ourselves had a Queen, and she had daughters. They tried argument with Rome, and then tried pleading. I want no other woman to try.'

A silence fell upon them, that Ban, to bring back ease, broke by turning to the King with a tale of an old serving-man — an old man who had been his father's servant — and now was troubled with a palsy. Did Glam, he asked, know of any remedy for his shaking?

'The smell of a fox,' said Glam. 'Catch a dog-fox, the older the better, and let him keep it in a box by his bed, and breathe the scent of it. That'll do him good, if anything will!'

'Good,' said Ban. 'I'll try that when I go home again. He shakes like a reed, but he's got all his wits about him still, and knows more old stories of the Fenland than any man alive.'

Then he held the table — Liss and Ferli and the young men alike — with stories of the river-fields and flat shores of Norfolk that were sometimes darkling fantasy and moonlit wonder; sometimes sharp and shrewd, of human waywardness and sudden laughter. He sloughed, or so it seemed, the hurry and sternness that war had given him, and now his face was genial and sly, or young and credulous — turn and turn about — as though he had lived all his life in a flat and stirring countryside and knew its gossip; but remembered too its sprites and dire enchantments. He brought rhymes and riddles to the table, a water-horse and a dishonest miller; and not till midnight did they see the soldier sitting there. But about midnight Liss said she must leave them; and Ban, grave again, stood up and thanked her, and took her hand.

'I am sorry,' he said, 'that love won't keep the Romans out, and let us go back to the old ways we knew before they came.'

'Love can give life,' she said, 'and give life again to what despairs. But love has no defences.'

'We haven't sunk to despair — not yet — and luck may serve us if love can't.'

'You are going to stay here, aren't you?'

'For a day or two, if you'll let me.'

'No more than that?'

'No more than that.'

He sat down again, and Albyn put a horn of mead into his hand. Never before had Albyn been so quiet at his own table, but all evening he had been content to listen, and still he wanted to hear more of Ban's tales. 'Drink,' he said, 'and tell us again about the Romans and your war.'

Ban looked round him, sipping his mead, and asked, 'Will it offend you if I boast a little?'

'Boast, in God's name!' said Albyn. 'Your manners are too good for us, and you needn't be so modest here in Galloway.'

Then Ban told them of the defeat of the Ninth Legion near Lincoln, and told it without bragging in spite of his plea for licence; but let them see how the Romans, hampered by their harsh discipline, had been overwhelmed by cunning, fierce, and swift manœuvre. He described some Roman officers in captivity, and their unbending gloomy dignity when the English, flushed and glorious with victory, pulled them into a ring and tried to make them dance. He mimicked their pompous dullness, told tales of tricking their solemnity, and made the power of Rome seem like a

thing of folly, and Roman conquest a bitter farce. —
But when Albyn went to bed, Liss was lying awake,
and said, 'You won't go away with him, will you?'

'With Ban?' said Albyn. 'Why should I go with
him?'

'You were watching him all night as a man watches
a girl that he's in love with.'

'I'm in love with no man,' said Albyn. 'I'm in love
with you.'

'Is it deep enough to hold you?'

'You're tired, or you've been dreaming,' said Albyn.
'And I'm tired too. It's late. Let's sleep.'

'Did you take my father home?'

'Yes, and against his will. If he'd had his way he'd
have sat talking to Ban all night.'

'He's on your side too. Your side and Ban's. Oh,
Albyn, I'm all alone!'

'Alone? When I'm here?'

'But how long?' cried Liss. 'How long?'

Ban, on the following morning, said he would like
to see something of the country before returning to
England, so he and Albyn rode to Glenluce, and
supped and slept with a cousin of King Glam, a very
dull old man with a young and lively wife — the third
he had taken — whose younger sister was livelier still.
In a small company of a dozen or so they grew genial
after supper, and Ban, who was now on easy terms
with Albyn, opened his heart about the private and
peculiar reasons he had for hating the Romans.

'War's war,' he said, 'and we can't really complain
because their drill's better than ours, and, on the whole
their tactics are better. But what I do complain about

is the advantage they take of their superiority. Their roads and their camps, for instance. — I've told you before how I dislike them. — They drive their roads straight across country, paying no attention to the look of the country and the wrong sort of attention to the look of the road. Now I think that's abominable! A straight road, I grant you, is the shortest distance from here to there; but does that help you to enjoy yourself on the way? Of course it doesn't! And when I go on a journey I want to enjoy myself. I want to look at the lie of the land, and be surprised when I turn a corner. A road, I say, should be tender to the country it crosses, and embrace it as gently as a good-hearted man embraces a pretty girl.'

'Of course it should!' cried the lively young sister of King Glam's dull cousin's lively young wife.

'And their camps,' said Ban, 'are sheer perversion. Squares and rectangles! Now what is there in nature that confines itself like that?'

'Nothing,' said Albyn, 'nothing at all. A square's a beastly thing.'

'The bee,' said King Glam's dull cousin, 'makes its comb of regular hexagonal cells, which appear to serve its purpose very comfortably.'

'And what in nature's more miserable than a drone?' asked Ban.

'The ant, perhaps,' said Albyn.

'The pismire and the bee,' said Ban, 'are the Roman legions in the world of insects. Daunted by drill, damned by efficiency, and slaves to a purpose that denies them happiness. The pismire lives only to work, and out of ten thousand bees there's only one — one only in ten thousand lovers — that ever consummates its love!'

'Oh, how horrible!' cried King Glam's dull cousin's wife and her young sister; and hurried to bring more mead.

'If the bees had their own way,' said a timid-looking man who had not spoken before, 'we might have less honey.'

'And is that any reason,' demanded Albyn, 'why Ban and his people should work to fill a Roman hive?' — He spoke so fiercely that the timid-looking man took his leave soon after, and the other guests went with him. King Glam's dull cousin fell fast asleep, and his wife and her sister listened with the greatest interest — though without much understanding — to a few more profound and eloquent assertions of the misery of the insect-world and the abomination of rectangles. The mead was good, and the dull husband, notoriously a heavy sleeper, snored as though he would never wake.

In the morning, somewhat later than they had expected, Albyn and Ban rode east again, and reached Wigtown in good time for supper. Liss had prepared a feast and summoned thirty guests. She welcomed Ban in a little speech that wished him well in his struggle against the Romans, and made it clear enough that he could expect no help from Galloway except good wishes. The feast was richly served, but the conversation was less warm than at their first supper or the supper in Glenluce. Ban spoke well, and said how grateful he was for the hospitality he had received; and bade goodbye, for he would be leaving again at break of dawn.

'His affairs are no concern of ours,' said Liss to

Albyn in their chamber. 'His battles with the Romans are far away. They don't affect us, and never can.'

'Who knows how far the Romans will come if no one stops them?' asked Albyn.

'Over the border hills, and through the forests, and across the Yorkshire moors? It's unthinkable!'

'Hills and forests don't keep a giant at home; and their discipline gives them the strength of giants.'

'You've been listening to Ban too long. Too long and too closely. You set store on everything he says.'

'In some ways, in hidden ways, we're alike; though his life has been very different from mine.'

'What of that?'

'He is making a story — such a man fighting against the legions — as if he were a poet. And I believe in good stories.'

'Isn't the story of the Blind Glen good enough for you?'

'That was made by love and the proper words. It was your love, and only the words were mine. But I've never believed that a poet should live on words alone —'

'Or find peace in love?'

'Love has no defences.'

'And no bonds either?'

'Oh, bonds so strong that they're a torment when you struggle with them. I've never loved you more than now —'

'Is it true, then? Are you going?'

'I'll come back.'

Face to his breast, Liss wept; and Albyn held her while she sobbed and shook. He tried to comfort her, but his pity did not change the resolution he had made; and presently she turned away from him, and after crying very bitterly for a long time, grew calm and said, 'I knew, from the beginning, that you would leave me.'

Softly, with gentle argument and the tenderest endearments, he tried to defend himself and prove that he could love and leave her too. His left arm lay about her, and presently under his hand he felt that the movement of her body was slower. Her mouth half-open, she was breathing deeply; fast asleep.

When the grey of morning showed through the window-slit he rose without waking her, and dressed, and went outside. He took food and drink from the hall, and the leather sling he had used to small avail in the battle of the Blind Glen. He broke his fast, and in the paddock below the house caught a good grey pony. In the oyster-light of dawn he saw Ban come out, a bannock of beremeal in one hand and a cup of ale in the other, his axe hanging by a thong from the hand that held the ale.

'Well?' asked Ban, brusque in the morning.

'I'm coming with you,' said Albyn.